Florence Warden

A Dog With A Bad Name

Vol. 2

Florence Warden

A Dog With A Bad Name
Vol. 2

ISBN/EAN: 9783337411930

Printed in Europe, USA, Canada, Australia, Japan

Cover: Foto ©Andreas Hilbeck / pixelio.de

More available books at **www.hansebooks.com**

A DOG WITH A BAD NAME.

BY

FLORENCE WARDEN,

AUTHOR OF

"THE HOUSE ON THE MARSH" AND "AT THE WORLD'S MERCY."

IN THREE VOLUMES.

VOL. II.

LONDON:

RICHARD BENTLEY AND SON,

Publishers in Ordinary to Her Majesty the Queen.

1885.

PRINTED BY WILLIAM CLOWES AND SONS, LIMITED, LONDON AND BECCLES.

A DOG WITH A BAD NAME.

CHAPTER I.

THE heavy mists of the April night had crept through the doors and windows of Waringham Hall, and deepened the gloom of the big, bare-looking rooms, when the death-cry of its master rang through the house, startling the two Misses Otway, as they sat in the drawing-room underneath, penetrating to the servants' hall, where the old servants sat cowering, on the alert for the unusual after the strange arrivals and surprises of the evening.

There was a horrible silence in the death-chamber for a few moments; only one of the three living occupants of it had any idea what

that last strange cry uttered by Sir Charles
might mean.   The old housekeeper, whose
gray, wan face bore the seal of some great
terror, was the most composed of the three ;
she disengaged the almost fainting Geraldine
from the lifeless arms that still held her, and,
turning to James, in whose ears the terrible cry
still rang, she whispered in her quivering old
voice—

"Won't you take her downstairs, sir ? "

He started, looked from the old woman to
the young one, and, touched by the girl's mute
misery, glad of something to do to dispel the
eerie feeling of a nameless horror, which in
him took the place of grief at the strange end
of the uncle who had never cared about him,
he led her gently from the room and down
the staircase.   But, though he held her arm
affectionately in his, and mechanically spoke
kind and soothing words to her, his mind was
occupied—now that the shock of the death-
scene was past—by a hundred strange and perplexing questions.   There was some mystery
here, of which perhaps that sudden death had
sealed the solution for ever.   Why, if his uncle

had expected to see him, as his calling him by
his name had seemed to indicate, had he experienced a shock so great at sight of him that
it was probably the immediate cause of his
death? And what was the meaning of his
calling Geraldine, in that earnest tone of deep
and joyful gratitude, his daughter, his own
child? It had not sounded like a vague term
of affection, that trembling, sobbing heart-cry;
it had struck James at once, as he heard it, as
raising a perplexing question, to which perhaps
now the answer would never be given. He
could see that neither of these mysteries occupied the girl on his arm, whose whole heart
and mind were entirely absorbed in her passionate grief. She was trying hard to keep
from crying, and her frame was trembling with
the effort; but the sobs would rise to her lips,
and, hang her head as she would, he could see
the tears falling.

"Don't cry, there's a dear," whispered he
gently, but ineffectually, as he stopped with her
at the foot of the staircase while she dried her
eyes. "He was very good, you know, wasn't
he? So he is sure to be all right," said he, in

a shy but soft attempt to administer religious consolation.

"Oh yes, I am not afraid of that! He was the best man that ever lived. You don't know how good he was!" she whispered earnestly, looking up with red swollen eyes which touched James, who was soft-hearted about women's tears, and did not notice, in his anxiety to comfort her, how they spoilt her pretty face.

"No," he said rather shortly. "I've no doubt he was very good to you—nobody could help it. But you should not be so miserable, Deldee dear; you know he can't have been very happy living here with my aunts!"

"Oh, James, how could he bear it?" she asked, a sudden sense of the marvellous stopping her tears for the moment, as she looked up at him with an awestruck expression of face.

"Heaven knows!" said he solemnly.

"What will they say? They don't know; you will have to tell them!"

"Yes. Would you mind coming in with me, Deldee? I can't leave you now, and I won't let them bite you, and—and, to tell you the truth, I would rather not face the hags alone. I don't know what they will do."

"Ye-es, I'll go in with you; only don't—don't let the hard one speak to me now, or I shall break down, or fly at her, or run away; I—I really couldn't bear it, if she were to—to begin again now!"

And the girl shuddered.

"What, has she attacked you already to-night? The she-devil!" he added below his breath. "No, don't be afraid; she shan't annoy you again."

So, fortified by their mutual support, the woman leaning on the man's strong arm, but communicating to him her own firm spirit, they entered the drawing-room together.

Elizabeth, who had followed James out of the library when he left her, was sitting on the sofa beside her sister, feeling for once the need of a human touch in the horror with which the piercing cry, whose significance she did not yet understand, had filled her. She looked up as the door opened, and her face contracted as her nephew and the girl she hated advanced up the room together. Something in their faces gave her warning before either spoke. She started up and tried to speak, but could not.

"How is Charles?" moaned the shivering Eleanor, whose head was half buried among the cushions of the sofa. "It was very unkind of you to let the doctor go away without seeing me. I want a doctor quite as badly as Charles does."

"Yes, aunt; uncle Charles will never want a doctor again."

She gave a little cry, and fell to moaning and weeping, while her sister, very quiet, very still, but with a fever of anxiety burning brightly in her hard eyes, went up to him, laid her hand on his arm, and beckoned him aside. He glanced at Deldee, who slipped away, and, kneeling down beside the poor down-broken old woman on the sofa, applied herself to comforting her as well as she could with smelling-salts and caressing hands. Elizabeth, meanwhile, led her nephew to the other end of the room.

"What was—the meaning of—that cry?" she asked, her voice not quite steady. "Was it—Charles?"

"Yes, it was the last sound my uncle uttered, and he uttered it on seeing—me. He seemed to know I was near, for he called me by my name; yet, when I appeared, he started up with the cry you heard, as if in terror; and then he fell back—dead. Can you explain this?"

It was very dark at the end of the room where they were standing; but James, who spoke slowly, with his eyes fixed upon his aunt's face, saw her first look of utter bewilderment give place to a glimmer of intelligence, as if a possible clue to the mystery—not by any means a full solution, but still a clue—had occurred to her.

"Can you think of any explanation?" he asked again, as she gave no answer to his first question.

"None," she replied, this time promptly.

And it was on her nephew's lips to tell her that she lied. As, however, this course would certainly have produced no good result, he checked himself, and only said rather drily—

"I am sorry you cannot help me, because there was another rather curious point upon which I had thought of consulting you."

Each maintained a guarded attitude, and the glances they exchanged at this moment were alight with mutual mistrust. Elizabeth turned towards him with an impulsive show of confidence.

"Don't force me to speak too soon, or I may spoil the value of what I only partly know by helping it out with wrong guesses. I have a suspicion, a very *strong* suspicion ; as soon as I make it a certainty, if I do make it a certainty, you shall know it. Now, what have you to tell me ?"

"Nothing. I have to ask you something. Who is Geraldine's father ?"

In spite of herself, Elizabeth started. He caught her arm.

"Quick—speak ! You do know something this time !"

"Yes, I do," she answered, recovering her serenity. "But it is something you will not like to hear."

"Never mind. But tell me the truth."

"Geraldine's father, I have every reason to believe, is Lindley Fielding."

"Lindley ! That scoundrel ! Impossible !"

cried James aloud, startling the two women at the sofa.

"Hush!" cried his aunt. "Don't shout so! She does not know."

"But it is not true. Good Heavens, I never heard such nonsense!"

"Why call it nonsense? Compare her face with his mother's portraits, and you will no longer say so. As for his character, that does not affect her, you know," she added, with something almost like eagerness in her voice.

"But what reason have you for supposing this? My uncle never thought so, I am sure."

"If you had been here for the whole of the last two days, and had seen Lindley, and heard the confident manner in which he talked, you would agree with me. He came here with the determination to persuade poor Charles to adopt the girl; you were no longer in the way to oppose such a project; the way was clear. We shall probably hear more of the matter in a few days, when Lindley appears, or gets some one to appear for him, with the will he professes to have seen Charles make."

James was silent for a few instants.

" It is a very extraordinary business," said
he at last, " and not quite so simple as you
describe, I fancy !   Surely, if the girl had been
Lindley's child, we should have heard something of this before.   Now, I have a different
theory to suggest, which accounts just as well
for her resemblance to Aunt Henrietta."

"And that is——" said Elizabeth, trying
to hide her deep anxiety.

" Well, I'll think it over, and tell you the
result of my reflections and inquiries.   In the
meantime, aunt, if only out of consideration for
my uncle's deep affection for her, I must beg
you to treat her kindly—I will even say I insist
upon it."

Elizabeth looked up at her nephew curiously.
He was assuming the airs of mastership very
promptly ; a great change seemed to have come
over him already since that interview in the
library, in which she had felt for the greater
part of the time that the reins were in her own
hands as surely as they had been when she was
dealing with her brother.   James was easily
led, as he had said ; but was it already decided
that it was not she who was to lead him ?   She

must prepare for a struggle for authority, she saw; in the meantime, dutiful and prompt submission was the best plan.

"There is no need to insist upon that point, James," she said quietly. "If poor Charles had not adopted the extraordinary plan of hiding her away from us, which of course puts out of the question the theory of a secret marriage which Lindley may try to set up, we should have opened our arms to the girl years ago. Now that you adopt the more sensible plan of appealing to our kindness, she shall have no reason to complain of her reception."

And, glad to close the *tête-à-tête*, Elizabeth straightway left him to follow her while she made her way to the sofa, and, pressing Geraldine gently down again as the girl tried to rise from the kneeling position in which she was still consoling Miss Eleanor, she said, in a tone which would have won the girl's heart but for that cruel scene of an hour ago which the elder lady seemed to have forgotten—

"Don't move, my child. We need all the sympathy your warm young heart can give us now."

And she put her slender white hand on
the girl's shoulder as [Geraldine instinctively
recoiled, and said in a low voice in her ear—

" I have been mad with anxiety and grief
this evening. If I said anything to pain you in
my paroxysm of sorrow when you so unexpectedly came upon us in our trouble, forgive
me, dear child. You cannot measure misery
like mine."

This was true ; but Geraldine found it
difficult not to shrink from her caresses, difficult
to tell the necessary courteous falsehood that
it did not matter. For she could not forgive
this woman whose cruelty had wrung her heart,
and whose handsome blue eyes remained hard
through her cooing conciliatory speeches. The
little selfish, groaning, exacting Eleanor, who
had unconsciously revelled in the attentions
and soft touch and soft speech of the young
girl, seemed an angel of light compared with
her still handsome and stately sister.

"Will you stay here to-night ? It is late
for you to return to Copsley, and I will myself
take you safely back to Miss Gretton to-morrow
morning," Elizabeth said solicitously, being

rather anxious for an opportunity of making
fuller amends to this hateful interloper, who
threatened, whatever course affairs might take,
to become a stronger power than ever at
Waringham.

"Oh no, thank you! Mrs. Bamber has
asked me to spend the night at the Vicarage,
and Mr. Reginald Bamber has promised—to
come and fetch me," said Geraldine rather
shyly.

"Reginald Bamber!" broke in James, in a
not altogether pleased tone. "Oh, does he loaf
about the Vicarage still? He is old enough to
be out in the world, I should think. Why, he
must be over thirty by this time!"

"Oh yes; he is in partnership with a pub-
lishing firm in New York!" said Geraldine,
eager to defend her friend from the charge of
loafing. "He is only here on a visit; he is
going back soon; he told me so."

"Oh!" said James. "And he is going to
take you to the Vicarage to-night? Oh, well,
I'll save him the trouble; I'll take you there
myself! The carriage will be round in a minute
to take me to the station, and I can drop you

on my way." He did not speak very good-
temperedly. Reginald Bamber and he had
never been very good friends ; Reginald never
quarrelled with anybody, and this fact had been
a constant source of irritation to James, who
was hot-tempered and strong-limbed, and had
always been rather fond, in his boyhood, of a
row with a fight as the climax. His ill-humour
increased when Geraldine said hesitatingly—

"I think I must wait for him, James, as he
promised. You see it was he who brought me
here."

" He brought you here ! How was that ? "

" He drove over to Copsley with a message
from—— " Her voice trembled ; she could
not pronounce the dear name again yet. " A
message to say I—was sent for."

Before James could add another question,
his aunt Elizabeth changed the subject.

" But surely, you are not going away to-
night, James ? She was getting more and more
puzzled as to the circumstances of his visit, and
yet none of them dared broach the subject with
him.

" Yes, I am," he answered obstinately,

"What should I stay here for? My spirits are low enough already, and my presence is not likely to raise yours much, I should think. I have a room at an hotel in Ipswich."

Once more the air of gloomy undecided restlessness, which the shock of the death-scene upstairs and the need of comforting Deldee had for a short time dispersed, was settling on him. Again his eyes were fixed vacantly upon the opposite wall, and his fingers played list-lessly with the antimacassar on the back of a chair in front of him. The three women looked at him shyly, their minds all filled with the same question. Before any one spoke again, the door-bell rang.

"Reginald Bamber, I suppose?" said Eliza-beth.

But it was not Reginald; it was his father, the Vicar. It was so long before any one was announced that James, growing impatient, went out into the hall and found Mr. Bamber divest-ing himself carefully of macintosh, muffler, respirator, and overshoes. It was a very exceptional event for him to go out at all after the evening dews had begun to fall; but he

had been anxious about his old friend Sir
Charles and the curious state of affairs up at
the Hall, and so had represented to his son
that it would be more proper for him to escort
Miss Lindley to the Vicarage himself. He had
just learnt the baronet's death and James's
arrival from the butler, and all he could find
breath to utter in his guttural sepulchral voice
was " Good gracious ! " He was saying it for
the fourth or fifth time as the young man came
out and greeted him.

" I'm very glad to see you, my dear boy ! "
said the Vicar, bewildered, shaking hands with
him cordially, however. " Come for—for a long
stay, I hope ? " he hazarded, hovering, as the
butler and every one else had hovered, between
the ideas of a ticket-of-leave and of escape.

James's answer suggested the latter as the
correct view.

" No, I'm going away already. This place
is a sepulchre for the living as well as the dead ;
I should go mad if I stayed here a week."

" But at such a time as this it would be
more becoming to stay—if you could manage
it," hinted the Vicar, knowing that an escaped

convict has other points besides his own con-
venience to consider.

" I have done with questions of conve-
nience," said James, shortly. " I don't know
what instinct made me come back here at all;
a much stronger one prompts me to get away
from it as fast as I can."

" And where are you going ?" asked the
Vicar, in a practical tone.

" I don't know, and I don't care. As far
away as I can get from every one who has
ever known me—to the bottom of the sea,
perhaps."

" Oh, nonsense!" said the Vicar, shaking
his head in much irritation. " A most absurd,
most unmanly idea. A misspent youth or a
fatal act cannot be retrieved at the bottom of
the sea."

James began to look sullen.

" There is no retrieval possible for me," he
said. " I'm ruined; done for. If I still stick
to life, it will not be to retrieve my own
faults, but to revenge myself on the man who
encouraged me to indulge in them."

" Dear me—most unchristian, most unchristian !" muttered the Vicar, shaking the moisture off his macintosh. " His errors, whatever they may be, are not your affair ; they will be more dispassionately considered in another quarter. You are a young man in the prime of your youth, with a strong pair of arms and a chest that I would give anything for. You have thrown away your position—well, get another. Take a spade and go to one of the colonies, as many a better and a better-born man too, for the matter of that, has done before you. What is the good of revenge ? It will only put you back again where you have just come from ; you will be exceedingly uncomfortable until you have got it, and a good deal more uncomfortable still afterwards. Take my advice, my dear boy, and give it up."

The Vicar had by this time taken off his overcoat and his woollen gloves, and turned down his trousers. James accompanied him as far as the drawing-room door, and there said—

" You will find my aunts and Miss—Miss— and Geraldine in there, Mr. Bamber. Will you excuse me while I go up and speak to the housekeeper? I have to catch a train to Ipswich to-night, and I must see Mrs. Symes before I go."

The Vicar, after a look at the gloomy vacant expression of the young man's face, felt strongly averse from letting him go; but, having no excuse to offer for detaining him, he was obliged to enter the drawing-room alone. His first remark, however, after he had offered his heartfelt condolences to the sisters, who were both sobbing now, while Geraldine sat, tearless and anxious, a little apart from the group, was—

"We must not forget the living in our grief for the dead, Elizabeth—that young fellow, your nephew, ought in my opinion to be watched."

At these words Geraldine started up, and, unnoticed except by the Vicar, crept to the door and made her escape into the hall. She had scarcely got to the staircase when she met Johnson coming out of the dining-room.

"Have you seen Mr. James, Johnson?" she whispered.

"I met Sir James just now, Miss Geraldine,"

corrected the butler respectfully, "on his way upstairs. He asked where Mrs. Symes was, as he desired to speak with her."

"Oh!" said she, hesitating. But Johnson was an old friend in whom she might confide; so, after a moment, she asked timidly, "Did he seem quite—quite calm, Johnson?"

"Oh yes, ma'am, he seemed calm enough— too calm to my thinking, considering we've just lost—the—the best of gentlemen!" quavered the old servant.

"He is too unhappy himself to feel it as keenly as we do, you know, Johnson," said she, not very steadily. "He is more to be pitied than any of us, I think. He says you used to be kind to him once; don't join the rest in being hard to him now."

"Well, he's got a better defender than me in you, ma'am!"

"Why, yes; don't you know that if it hadn't been for him, I should never have seen—seen him again," she went on earnestly; "that he brought me in and led me upstairs himself? Oh, I would forgive him anything, anything in the world, just for that!"

"It does seem strange, Miss Geraldine, don't it, that both times it should have been Master James that brought you into Waringham Hall—a sort of fate-like, ma'am, if one was superstitious?"

"Both times! What do you mean, Johnson?" asked the girl, suddenly trembling.

He saw that he had gone too far. If the grief and the surprises of the evening had not played havoc with his usual discretion, he would never have let slip that unlucky remark. Her interest once roused by such a question as that, nothing but the truth would content her; and, as she let him know that she had learnt part of the truth about her parentage, he at last most reluctantly told her that it was Master James who had found her—he declined to say where —but who had brought her to the hall nineteen years ago, and had thus been the means of introducing her to Sir Charles. She listened without a word of comment, or any other sound than an occasional faint sob, as the tears rained down her cheeks.

"And now Master—Sir James will be most dreadfully angry with me for telling you, Miss

Geraldine; but it slipped out somehow—I don't know how—in spite of myself."

"He shall not be angry with you, Johnson," the girl assured him, taking the old servant's hand in hers. "Or, even if he is at first, you shall not suffer for this, I promise you. You have rendered me a service I shall never forget."

"Thank you, ma'am," said he, reverentially, much impressed by the resolute dignity with which the young lady spoke.

And he retired, leaving her still standing in the hall, at the bottom of the carved oak staircase, looking mechanically at the great pictures on the walls, with her head and her heart in a tumult of new thoughts, new feelings. When at last she heard James's footsteps in the corridor above, she felt her limbs trembling and a choking sensation in her throat, which warned her that she would find it difficult to keep her voice under control.

He came lounging down with an angry, disappointed expression of face. He had questioned the old housekeeper searchingly concerning the events of the evening; but she had answered him in a manner which impressed him

with the conviction that she had been skilfully
tampered with, and that she was in possession
of important facts which nothing he could say
would induce her to disclose. By nature rather
a slow-witted, stupid woman, she had by some
means been persuaded or threatened into that
strongest of safeguards, silence ; and it appeared
that whatever events of interest had taken place
in the course of the evening had occurred while
she was "in the next room." But, in the face
of this mechanically given excuse, the leaden
colour her features had assumed, the stiff con-
traction of the deep lines round her eyes and
mouth, bore witness to some great terror
through which she had passed, which had set
its seal upon her for the rest of her days. So
that, baffled in his inquiries, oppressed by the
mystery which deepened tenfold the gloom of
the death-stricken household, he descended the
stairs, anxious to get out of the place as quickly
as possible.

"Johnson, Johnson, is the phaeton round
yet ?" he called, in an instinctively subdued
voice as he came down, hearing a sound in the
hall below him.

But it was not the butler who came forward
out of the shadow as he reached the bottom
step; it was Geraldine.

"Oh, James, you are not going!" she cried,
as she seized his hand. "Don't go while
you are so unhappy—don't; I can't bear the
thought of it. You must stay and hear what I
have to say; you must stay and let me thank
you—I have only just found out what I have to
thank you for."

"Why, what is that?" asked he very gently,
utterly bewildered by the passionate gratitude
which shone in her face and thrilled her low
voice, and made the touch of her fingers electric
with deep feeling.

"Everything, everything — my guardian's
love and care and kindness—everything that has
made my life worth living—everything but life
itself. Oh, James, have you forgotten what
you did for me nineteen years ago?"

"Deldee, who has told you?" he asked,
taking her hands, and looking with swimming
eyes into the girl's face.

"Never mind; I know. It was you who
brought me to Waringham; it was you who

took me out of poverty; it was you who gave
me to—him! It was you, wasn't it?"

"Yes," replied James in a low voice; "it
was I, Deldee. You were hardly more than a
baby, and a very naughty baby too, when I
found you and fell in love with you and carried
you off, nineteen years ago. I thought you
were a fairy, and so did my uncle. There was
quite a fight between us and some other people
as to who should have you; and you came of
your own accord to my uncle and me. He was
superstitious about you, and thought you would
bring luck to Waringham; but it would indeed
take a fairy to do that."

"Did he think that, James?" she asked in
a whisper, with fiery earnestness in her dark
eyes. "That I was a fairy—that I could bring
luck to people?"

"So you will, my child, to some man; you
will bring all the luck and all the happiness
that a man can enjoy to—to Reginald Bamber,
perhaps!" he ended bitterly.

"No, James," said she earnestly, while a
deep flush rose into her face; "not to Reginald
Bamber. I know what you mean; but you are

wrong. Fairies don't marry, and I shall not marry; but I shall not go away to live in the clouds ; I shall stay to live the life of a woman here in the world, but with only one thought, only one determination—to repay some day— I don't know when, I don't know yet quite how —the debt of all I owe to you."

The earnestness and fire of the girl as she made this strange declaration, with the dreamy poetry of a child, and yet with the passionate intensity of a woman, kept James for a few moments silent, reading dimly in her eyes the story of what the rash impulses of an ill-spent youth had lost him.

" It is too late, Deldee !" he cried at last hoarsely. " Nothing your warm, generous heart could feel for me, nothing your sweet little hands could do for me, can help me now."

"You don't know," she answered resolutely, her great eyes, shining with strange faith, meeting his solemnly. " You can't guess what I can do, because I have spent my life quietly, without anything serious to occupy me. You think, because I am only a woman, that it is quite funny to hear me talk of doing anything

more important than wool-work. But I have
energies and powers that no one knows of yet;
and Heaven will increase them and strengthen
them tenfold if I use them in the right way, to
fulfil a vow I have made to-night."

She spoke like a prophetess; but James
was naturally more moved by the warmth of
her tones than by the impulsive words themselves.

"You shouldn't make vows, Deldee, especially about ne'er-do-weels," said he very tenderly. "I am not worth one throb of your
tender little heart."

"Ah, you talk to me as if I were a child; but
you will know better some day! And you
can't prevent my vow, because it is made," she
said, with naïve solemnity. "And, however
much you may laugh at me and my simplicity
now, I shall keep it; and some day, when you
are in trouble—and you have just the nature
that slips into trouble easily—I have found that
out already—and when you are at your wits'
end for a friend to help you, you will find the
fairy you laughed at by your side, James,
without the aid of any magic ring to call her."

" Heaven forbid that I should laugh at
you !" said James, who indeed had tears in his
eyes. "Why, my dear little fairy, you have
done more than you think for me already! If
it hadn't been for you, I—I—— Never mind."

He was holding her hands, wringing them
in his with a firm pressure, while he kept his
eyes away from her face.

" And you won't do anything foolish or—or
wrong, that would hurt you, will you? You
know it would be so unkind to me when I
should care so much!" she added appealingly.

" I can't promise never to do anything foolish
or wrong, Deldee my child, because in that case
I should have to change James Otway's identity
for somebody else's. But I promise to trust in
you as my good fairy, and to believe that this
soft hand, which looks, as you suggest, only fit
for doing wool-work, is really a hand of iron
strong enough to help those it befriends out of
any danger, any difficulty. It led me pretty
nearly where it liked in the old days; so why
not now ?"

He spoke playfully ; but the girl took every
word in earnest in spite of him. She did not

resent his jesting tone, knowing very well that
her words had a deeper effect upon him than
he chose to show. How deep she scarcely
guessed even when they were suddenly interrupted by the appearance of Johnson, who, on
being called back, as he was discreetly retreat-
ing, announced that the phaeton was at the
door; and James said briefly—

"Send it back again. I shall stay here to-
night."

Geraldine was not sure whether she was
glad or sorry—glad, because he was not going
to rush away from his home and his evident
duty to his uncle's memory and his aunts'
wishes; or sorry, because he would, in his
dangerously despondent state, be still further
depressed by this gloomy house with its weird
occupants, dead and living. Besides, she did
not even know whether he was safe from
pursuit. Her fingers trembled in James's hand,
as he gave the order and led her slowly to the
drawing-room. The Vicar was much relieved
to see that the young man looked less melancholy, but could not approve of the means by
which this change had been brought about, for

he took a genuine interest in the welfare of
pretty modest Geraldine Lindley and gave his
warmest approval to his son's suit.   He hurried
her off very quickly; but, while Johnson was
helping him on with his voluminous protective
apparatus against the night-air, James led the
young girl into the outer hall and stood beside
her, looking down upon her very eloquently,
but with nothing to say.   Just as the Vicar's
rattling voice was heard thanking the butler
through his respirator, Geraldine whispered
timidly—

" James, are you safe here ? "

And, looking down at her with a sudden
change of face, while a quiver ran through his
frame, he answered with passionate earnestness,
the meaning of which she did not rightly
interpret—

" No."

CHAPTER II.

GERALDINE awoke next morning at the Vicarage, oppressed, unhappy, anxious as she had never been before. Reginald was called into the study by his father as soon as breakfast was over ; and Mrs. Bamber, who had household duties to attend to, and who was not without an intention of preparing a *tête-à-tête* between her son and the pretty guest, sent Geraldine into the garden.

At first the girl thought she was glad to be alone ; at all times fond of solitude, she had suddenly felt, while on her knees listening to Reginald's sweet voice as he intoned family prayers, that she must break away and escape somewhere to indulge in a wild fit of crying ; and at breakfast she had only been able to keep

her self-control by speaking as little as possible.
But, once out in the garden, free to hide herself
in the winding paths that were concealed from
view from the house by hedges of tall evergreens, the longing to cry suddenly left her,
and gave place to a heavy melancholy that was
harder still to bear; and then her loneliness
began to distress her, and she paused at the
garden gate to look out over the field beyond,
and up to the left towards the church, behind
which one could just see the first trees of Waringham Park. And she stood there as quietly
as a statue, and waited and listened. And very
soon she heard a man's footsteps, and she
started, and the colour deepened in her face.
Before she saw any one, however, she knew
that it was Reginald Bamber sauntering up
from the house; she looked to right and left
for a path down which to escape ; but, before
she had gone many steps very softly between
two yew hedges, his musical voice, which
irritated her this morning, said—

" Have you lost your way in this labyrinth,
Miss Lindley ? "

" No ; I was trying to find—wondering if

I could see a—a way out," said she foolishly, without quite knowing what she felt ashamed of.

" Let me help you."

He came to her side, and walked with her, and gathered her some lilac, and said sympathizing things, and was very kind.

But all the time she was ungratefully thinking that the perfectly suitable and correct condolences he made sounded stereotyped and soulless, and the sweet voice in which he made them irritated her spirit instead of soothing it. When he spoke of James—kindly, but with the implied unquestionable superiority to which his own blameless character gave him a right—she felt her teeth clenching, while a wild impulse sprang up in her to throw the lilac he had given her over the hedge and to answer him savagely, and to do half a dozen other unladylike things to express her sudden unreasonable anger. At last, when he, never guessing what a tempest he was raising, suggested that it was rash of James to venture to come to the Hall, especially at such a time, she burst out—

" You would not have had him keep away from the Hall at such a time, would you ? "

Reginald looked down at her in surprise, which made her blush.

"I did not know that he came to see Sir Charles because he was ill; I thought his arrival at such a time was quite accidental," said he gently. "His coming does more credit to his affections than to his prudence."

Now Geraldine knew that it did credit neither to the one nor the other; so she kept silence. Thinking the subject was distasteful to her, he proceeded to change it by asking, as a pet spaniel of his mother's came running along the path towards them, whether she was fond of dogs.

"Yes," she replied. "I think I shall ask James—Sir James—to let me have old Noel; I don't suppose the Misses Otway will want him, and Sir James would give him up to me, I know."

Noel was an old Newfoundland, which had been a great favourite with Sir Charles. This remark seemed to invite a return to the subject of the new master of the Hall.

"What is he going to do?" asked Reginald, in a puzzled tone. "I don't yet understand his coming at all. You see," he went on, lowering his voice, "although they managed to keep it dark to a great extent, rumours have got about the place concerning the reason of his long absence; and the least mystery about a man is clue enough for the police—if they want him. He has been very reserved, hasn't he? My father says he never alluded to—to the manner of his coming at all, except indirectly, by seeming anxious to be off. Has he said anything about it to you?"

"No—o, nothing," she answered very quietly, but in terrible anxiety which she did her best to hide.

"And he is so dreadfully rash—unless he has really been released. William, the postman, told me this morning that last night he met two men who told him Mr. James Otway had come back, and was none the better for his stay in foreign parts. It seems that the night before they saw him at an hotel in Ipswich very much intoxicated. Can you imagine anything more imprudent for a man in his position?"

Imprudent! That was the man's view.

To the girl this revelation was full of unutterable horror.

"Sir James's refined habits and manners don't interest me!" said she coldly.

"Of course not," quickly assented Reginald, who would not have thought of insulting this girl, who to him was a pearl among women, by supposing her capable of feeling any but the most distant and disdainful interest in such a man as James Otway had evidently become. "But I am sure you must feel that it is a sad thing to see a man's life wrecked, even if it is by his own fault; and one must make allowance for the utter disorganization which follows an experience of that kind in any but the best-balanced minds."

This speech brought tears to her eyes, not tears of sympathy, but of vexation and anger, against whom she hardly knew. She almost thought that it was against Reginald, when the sudden appearance of James Otway at the gate, which they were now again approaching, made her instantly aware that her anger and bitter disgust were for him. He did not look pleased on seeing her with Reginald; but his face and

voice fell into sweetness as he took her hand.
But she was cold as ice, cold as his aunts, this
morning.

"I am quite well, thank you," she answered
stiffly to his affectionate inquiry.

Reginald was quite distressed by her unkindness to a man who, whatever his faults and
crimes might be, was after all an old friend in
misfortune. He took the unwilling hand of the
prodigal, who had drawn back deeply hurt, in
a warm and hearty grasp, and said—

"So glad to see you back, old man! Come
in ; my mother is impatient to see you."

But James said—

"Thanks, no—awfully busy—got a lot to
do! Only looked in just to—just to see you,
and tell you I'm off again. Good morning."

He raised his hat to Geraldine without
looking at her, and was gone before a sound
could pass her lips. Reginald ran after him,
and the girl was left standing very still, with
remorse and a deep yearning pity in her heart.
Reginald looked almost stern as he came more
slowly back again.

"What is the matter with him?" she asked
quite coolly.

" Indeed I cannot tell, if you cannot, Miss Lindley."

" He has picked up very strange manners—er—wherever he has been to."

Reginald looked at her in a very much puzzled way, and laughed a little.

" Ladies are very difficult to understand, Miss Lindley. They are supposed to be tender-hearted, and yet—— Have you any idea how cruel you are ? "

" Cruel ! I only made a very natural remark. Did you ever see such strange behaviour ? But perhaps he is not sober."

" Miss Lindley, have some mercy ! I—I—you really—— " He stammered for a moment, but then said, " Don't you really know why the poor fellow went off so suddenly ? "

" Indeed I cannot imagine any reason strong enough to send a sane man rushing off like a lunatic."

" Shall I tell you what he said when I overtook him ? "

" If it is anything worth hearing, which I doubt."

" I cannot tell you the exact words he used,

because allowance has to be made again—I am afraid a good deal of allowance has to be made for poor Otway. But it was something to this effect—that he would rather be in—well, in very unpleasant circumstances than—er—face a lady who could be so unkind to him."

The words stabbed the girl ; but she only shrugged her shoulders slightly, and said—

" How absurd !"

And Reginald, although he had no idea how deep her feeling was, came . to the right conclusion that she was sorry for her coldness ; and he thought she did not like to own her pity for so contemptible an object of it. She expressed a wish, almost feverish in eagerness, to return to Copsley, alleging how great Miss Gretton's anxiety must be ; and, as he drove her back, she talked so much and in such a lively manner that he was rather shocked by such a strange demeanour on the morrow of a grief so deep as the death of her guardian.

He would have been reassured as to her depth of feeling if he could have seen her, after the briefest possible announcement to Miss Gretton of the events of her absence, locked

in her own room, lying on the floor in a
convulsion of mad grief, which distorted her
features and shook her frame and raged in her
whole being, until every faculty seemed shattered ; and she crept back again to fulfil her
duty of accompanying Miss Gretton in her
morning walk—now taken in the garden—with
dull, dizzy brain and tottering limbs and a great
void at her heart that nothing could fill.

Dull despair at her loneliness, and at the
impossibility of helping James or of saving him
from the misery and danger which seemed on
all sides to hem him in, had seized and paralyzed
her since her passionate outburst of grief an
hour ago ; and this state of apathy lasted all
through that day and to the afternoon of the
following, when it was destroyed by a most
unexpected event.

For, as the two ladies were sitting together
in the drawing-room, the elder dozing, the
young one neglecting the work in her hands to
stare in front of her with mournful, tearful eyes
which saw nothing, they were both suddenly
startled by the sound of wheels and hoofs, and
by the sight of the Otway barouche at the

door. With a thrill of joy which shattered her dull apathy in a moment, Geraldine heard James's voice; and, a few seconds later, he, with his aunt Elizabeth, entered the room, to the overwhelming astonishment of its occupants. For, although they knew each other by sight, it was the first time in all these years that the two elder ladies had met each other. With the boldness of youth, James had persuaded his aunt to take a step which his more timid uncle had never dared to suggest. They were profusely civil to one another, each showing off her grand manners, each too making an unexpectedly favourable impression upon the other; for Miss Otway and the twenty-years-older Miss Gretton, though women of entirely different dispositions, had intellects of equal keenness. The two younger members of the quartet were strangely shy with each other, and did very little talking, devoting themselves to watching the encounter between their elders. Elizabeth explained, with a stately and cold expression of grief, that she had thrown aside ceremony in coming at a time when they were all suffering from a great sorrow, at the request

of her nephew, who had begged her to give
her poor aid in entreating Miss Gretton to
allow her ward to return to Waringham Hall
with them for a few hours to comfort her sister
Eleanor, who was in a state of depression which
caused them great alarm, and who had taken a
strong fancy to the young girl. So Geraldine,
with the dignified permission of her old instructress, returned with Miss Otway and her
nephew to the Hall, rather silent, rather reserved, but inexpressibly comforted to find that
James, who was as silent and reserved as she,
had done nothing rash in his despondency.

But, as soon as they arrived at the Hall,
James, instead of letting her go to comfort his
eldest aunt, which was the ostensible reason of
her coming, whispered, as he helped her out of
the carriage—

"Will you come and see him?"

She assented; and he led her through the
dark halls, which made her shiver with dismal
recollections of two nights ago, up the staircase,
and into the solemn death-chamber where the
coffin lay. But the only sight in it that made
her shudder was the face of the housekeeper

watching there, whose thin, shrivelled features, stamped with an undying terror since the night of her master's death, impressed the girl with unreasonable terror, and made her shrink back on first entering the room.

"Would you rather not see him?" whispered James, offering to lead her back.

She conquered herself, and approached the coffin. But the first glance at the still waxen face she so deeply loved lying in the flood of bright afternoon sunlight which streamed through the white blinds, calmed her and drew from her eyes tears which were scarcely sorrowful at all. She kissed the cold forehead with reverent love; and when she left the room, after a long, long last look at the peaceful face which impressed her, in spite of her reason, with the feeling that he was only sleeping, and that the touch of his child's lips could affect him still, the ghastly horror of death which she had felt since she last visited the room had passed away.

"Come into the garden," whispered James; and, without waiting for an answer, he led her through the dining-room to the scantily filled

conservatory, and through that into the garden
outside. But he did not stop there. He could
see that she was in no mood for talking; so in
silence he led her through the paths on the
opposite side of the house to that of the
principal entrance, and through a low iron gate,
under the trees of the park, which extended
very little farther in this direction; then through
another gate, and across a road into a meadow,
at the other side of which they found a rough
cart-track which they followed.

"Where are you taking me?" asked Geraldine at last.

"Over the road we travelled together nineteen and a half years ago, Deldee."

She started, and he stopped.

"I thought, you know, Deldee, that, since
you have heard so much, it is better you
should learn everything about yourself that it is
possible to find out, and that we had better
begin by questioning the Corbyns, in whose
farmyard I first found you. But, if you don't
feel strong enough for the ordeal of investigation,
we'll go back, dear."

"No, no; you are quite right. Let us go
on," said she firmly.

So they went on in the April afternoon
sunshine across the meadow, skirted the pine-
wood where James used to play truant in com-
pany with Tip the terrier, and saw through the
slender tree-trunks the blue haze rising from
the lower ground beyond; and then they came
to the farmyard, and to the old shed with the
chickens and the ducks flocking about it just as
they used to do; and there in the corner stood
a red waggon which might have been the very
one under whose shafts James had found Deldee.
He looked in and began to laugh.

"I suppose you don't remember this place,
Deldee?" said he curiously.

"No."

"Well, I do. It was just in this corner
that I found you sitting on the ground on a
sack, and—— Hallo, Mrs. Corbyn, don't you
recognize two old friends?" he cried out,
shaking hands with her.

"I remember you, of course, sir, and I'm
very glad to see you back; but——"

"But you don't remember the lady I carried
off from you one October evening?"

Mrs. Corbyn started, and curtseyed as

Geraldine shook hands with her. She had exchanged the comeliness of her youth for that of mature age; but the expression of her face was as kind and good-humoured as ever. But through all the admiration for her transformed favourite which her shy glances betrayed, James saw that something was puzzling or distressing the farmer's wife; and, while Geraldine was engaged in caressing an ugly mongrel which came jumping about her, having taken a fancy to her, Mrs. Corbyn drew him a little on one side and said—

"It is the strangest thing in the world that you should bring the young lady here to-day, sir. Yesterday a gentleman came making inquiries about her, and saying he was her father."

Geraldine caught these words, and came quickly up, just as James was trying to silence the farmer's wife.

"No; go on please," she said quietly.

And Mrs. Corbyn, glancing from the one to the other, obeyed.

"He—he described the—the lady who brought you here, exactly, miss, so that I could

see her again as he spoke, and he said she was
his wife, whom he had been forced through
difficulties to leave for a time; and he said—
he said he was a cousin of poor Sir Charles's,
sir, and his wife knew that, and so brought the
child, when she herself got badly off; and, not
daring to take it up to the Hall herself, she left
it here with a letter, which, you, miss, being
very little and not understanding the importance of it—which you went and swallowed,
miss."

The girl looked incredulous; but James
confirmed the statement by a grave nod. Questioned further, the description Mrs. Corbyn
gave of the gentleman left no possibility of
doubt that it was Lindley Fielding, as both the
young man and the girl had at once feared.
This story alarmed them both. There was a
troubled pause in the conversation when they
had learnt all they could, which was broken by
the arrival of the farmer himself, on whom the
sight of his wife's visitors made a deeper impression than it had made upon her. He
guessed sooner than his wife had done who
the lady was; but, after examining her well, he

said, in a tone which frankly intimated his
opinion that she had not lived up to her early
promise——

"Ah, miss, you were a pretty little mite, if
ever there was one! I would have given my
head to have brought you up as my own."

"You were not so amiable about it then, if
I remember rightly," suggested James.

"Never you mind, Sir James! It sounds a
liberty to say it, now you've grown into a fine
lady," continued he, with an undercurrent of
pity for her degradation; "but I never took to
a child, before or since, not even to my own, as
I did to you, miss."

His wife tried to check the exuberance of
his reminiscences, thinking they might not be
agreeable to the lady's ears. But Geraldine
liked the farmer's blunt straightforwardness,
and encouraged him by thanking him for his
good intentions towards her.

"Well, I would have brought you up to the
best of my means, and you should have wanted
for nothing—in reason," he added prudently.
"I dare say you think you have done better
than that," he admitted. "But there is no

knowing—you have your life before you yet, and there's ups and there's downs. And if you ever should want the help of a plain man that's not a gentleman, but that has a few pounds at his back and a good roof over his head, you're welcome to come to me, madam, not for the sake of the fine lady you've grown into, but for the sake of the little creature that, by-the-by, I remember didn't take to me much nineteen years ago."

"Thank you," said Geraldine, touched by the genuine ring of the only half-gracious words. " Perhaps I appreciate you better now than I did then, to balance your evident preference for the baby over the ' fine lady.' "

Mr. Corbyn laughed constrainedly, and left his wife with her, in order to speak to the young gentleman, whom he led straight into the farmyard, well out of hearing of the women, before he unburdened his mind.

" I'm the last person to wish to interfere in anybody else's affairs, sir," he began ominouslly " But, at the same time, as a tenant for years of your late uncle, Sir Charles, and now of yours, sir, I am bound to feel an interest in the family—that you will understand, sir ; and stories have got about these last three days somehow—I don't wish to give offence ; but I have something to tell you which may be of service to you. This sudden illness and death of Sir Charles and your sudden arrival, and Mr. Fielding's goings on have set folks talking."

" And what do they say ? "

" Oh, goodness knows, sir ; a lot of cock-and-bull stories for the most part, and I only mention them because, if it hadn't been for all this commotion, I shouldn't have thought much of what I saw ! "

" And that was—— "

" A man looking about the Hall, sir, yester-day and to-day, after no good, I'll swear."

" My industrious relative, Mr. Lindley Field-ing, I expect, on vulture's business."

" No, sir, not Mr. Fielding."

" Who then ? "

" I don't know, Sir James. A man I never saw before."

James looked uneasy, though he tried to laugh the matter off.

"Thanks, Corbyn; I'll have the strong room watched."

But the farmer guessed, as the gentleman knew, that the man on the watch by Waringham Hall had not come after the plate.

CHAPTER III.

GERALDINE and James returned towards the
Hall, anxious and unhappy—at first each tried
to hide from the other this fact ; but the attempt
was a failure, and at last she said in a low
voice—

" Oh, I hope it is not true ! I have met the
man, and I don't like him."

James stopped.

" It is not true. Be sure, whatever happens, not to let any one persuade you that it
is. That man, under another name, has been
my ruin ; for some reason or other, he is now
working to effect yours. If you have any trust
in me, any care for your own happiness, don't
have anything to do with him. Believe me,
child, I speak from experience so bitter that, if
I were to live for a hundred years, I could not

outlive the effects ˉof it—he has wrecked me
body and soul."

" What has he done ? " she asked timidly.

" It is not a story for your ears, child ; it
would shock you, disgust you ; and all I want
is to warn you against falling into his hands.
He is a plausible scoundrel, and can cheat himself as well as the rest of the world. His love
of pleasure and of his own ease he mistakes
for philanthropy, and he is constantly complaining, in all good faith, of the unkind feelings
cherished against him by the victims of his
own rogueries. Promise, for my sake, that you
will have nothing to do with him."

" I can promise you that I don't want to do
so," she answered simply.

She had no fear of what this monster of
iniquity, as James described him to be, might
do to her ; she instinctively knew that life had
no dangers for her compared with those it had
for her stalwart companion. The disgust she
had felt at Reginald's revelations of the manner
in which James had spent the evening before
his return home had struggled vainly against
the affection for him which had never died out

since her childhood, and the gratitude which
had sprung up in her heart on learning that it
was to his childish fancy for her that she owed
her guardian's care and love through all these
years. This fact gave the young man a right
to reverence in her eyes, and she was now far
more ready to accuse herself for her ungrateful
coldness the day before than him for his vices
or his crime ; and she ingenuously thought it
was very good of him to bear no malice for that
snub of the morning previous. So she walked
along by his side, enjoying a subdued and timid
happiness in his society, until they reached the
park ; and James, not wishing yet to exchange
that pleasant *tête-à-tête* for the more restrained
intercourse of indoors, asked her if she would
like to come round the garden. She assented
willingly, yet with hesitation; evening was
closing in, and she had dragons to fear both
at Waringham Hall and Copsley. James led
her round to the front entrance, and to the
gate opposite, through which she had run to
escape him on his first appearance. They now
went through together, and sauntered along the
box-bordered path between two broad beds full

of bush-roses breaking into leaf, and lilac in
full blossom ; while guelder-roses, syringa, and
laburnum gave faint promise of later beauty,
and the petals of the already-fading almond-
blossom strewed the ground at their feet.
Geraldine was delighted with the charm of this
nook, and pained by the thought that she had
never been there with her guardian. James
saw the shadow cross her face, and to divert
her thoughts he said—

" It is not quite so pretty as the Vicarage
garden, is it ? And we have no lilac half so
fine as that I saw in your hands yesterday."

" It was very lovely ; Mr. Reginald Bamber
gave it to me," she answered, not without a
spontaneous impulse of mischief.

" Ah, I suppose you wouldn't look at a
flower of my gathering after that ! " said he,
with, however, no very wild display of jealousy.

" Oh, I might look at it, for the sake of the
flower ! I like flowers," said she demurely.

And she accepted a handful of little scentless
white Scotch roses, with carelessness which gave
no intimation of the care with which they were
to be treasured up.

"You are very hard, aren't you?" whispered James, as he rearranged them in her hands and tried to look into her eyes.

"What do you mean by 'hard'?" she asked in a low voice, after a pause of a few moments.

"Why, weren't you very unkind to me yesterday morning?"

Her breath came quickly, but at first she did not answer; then she said almost in a whisper—

"Please forgive me. They had been telling me shameful stories about you."

"'They' means Reginald Bamber, I suppose?" said he angrily. "And what stories did he tell you?"

"Oh, no, no, don't be angry; he only said— he said you were—I don't like to say it—I assure you I don't believe a word of it, James— Sir James; but he said—— "

"Well, what did he say, Miss Lindley?"

"No, don't call me that. He said, James, that you were—intoxicated at Ipswich the other night."

"Oh, is that all?" slipped out involuntarily.

Geraldine looked up at him in speechless horror. He could not help laughing.

"It is all right, Geraldine—at least, I mean it was very wrong. But if you knew how wretched I was, you wouldn't be so hard on me."

She had shrunk into herself in disgust. His crime of six years ago seemed nothing by comparison with this recent breach of propriety. She turned to go back to the house; but he gently detained her.

"Are you going to leave me again to be lonely and wretched so soon?"

"You can find better ways of consoling yourself than any I can invent," she began coldly.

But as he turned abruptly away, with an air suggestive of an intention to take her at her word, she sprang after him and put her hand on his arm remorsefully, pleadingly, her eyes full of tears.

"Oh, don't be angry; I am so sorry! Of course I have no right to interfere with you. And men look upon these things differently, I dare say. Forgive me, please; remember

how quietly and strictly I have been brought
up; if I knew more about the world, I dare
say I should not be shocked at all."

James looked in her face for a long time;
then he said, in a rather unsteady voice—

"No; that is true; however, if it is any
comfort to you to know it, I shan't try to con-
sole myself that way again—at least, to the
extent I have done sometimes," he added
prudently.

She pressed his hand silently and gratefully,
as if he had rendered her some service too
great to be acknowledged in words. He was
touched, though he did not want to show it.

"You are tired; shall we go in?" he asked.
"Just come into the grass-walk first; there is
something very pretty I have to show you
there."

He was right. Leaving the rose-corner by
another gate at the end of the path, they passed
under the low-bending ragged branches of a
great cedar, and into a broad grass-path, bordered by very high, thick hedges of laurels and
other evergreens. About fifty yards from the
beginning of this walk, the bordering shrubs

and trees grew thinner on the left-hand side,
and, forcing a passage through them, James led
Geraldine to a large pond, which they came
upon so suddenly that, as she found herself at
the edge of it, she gave a start and uttered a
faint cry of something more than surprise.
For the evening mist which already hung over
the black water, the beeches and slender white-
stemmed larches which grew closely round it
on all sides to its very brink, gave it in the dusk
a look of mystery which impressed her imagination. A smooth carpet of green duckweed
stretched over more than half of it, and at one
end an old water-logged boat, black in the dim
light, was moored by a slimy and rotten rope
to a stump, which rose slanting out of the sleek
green surface of the water.

"Pretty!" she remarked, with a shiver.
"I don't like it—at least, not now."

The romantic desolation of the spot, which
would have charmed her at another time, seemed
at this moment to revive all the sensations of
gloom and horror which she had experienced
in the last few days ; and James found it necessary to throw his arm round her, lest, in her

nervous agitation, she should slip into the pond.

"Oh, I'm not going to faint!" said she simply. "I never do."

But, as it is better to be on the safe side of a danger, he very kindly supported her until they were under the cedar tree again. It was very dark there; and, as she disengaged herself from his arm, not at all harshly, she could scarcely see his face, or he hers. But, at that very moment, he felt her tremble.

"What is it, Deldee dearest? You see you are not so strong-minded as you pretend."

She laughed, and said she supposed she was not; and she took his arm of her own accord, and talked fast and almost incoherently until they reached the house. As he rang the bell, she put her hand earnestly upon his shoulder.

"James," she said—and her eyes were wide and her voice was shaking—"don't laugh at me, but believe me! You are not safe here—I am sure of it!"

Before he could ask her what she meant, the door was opened, and they were scarcely in the Hall before Elizabeth met them.

"James," said she, "Mr. Bamber is here. He wishes particularly to see you."

"All right," he responded; "I will come and see him in a minute. Geraldine, come here; I want to show you the library."

His aunt, still adhering to her plan of opening the campaign by the most perfect feminine submission to him, retreated, and Geraldine let him lead her into the library, where, with a perceptible start, she recognized the tiger-skin rug which had struck her childish fancy and remained in her memory ever since her first introduction to Waringham Hall.

"Deldee," began James, recalling her to the present in a low voice—his right hand was playing idly with the papers on the table, and his eyes were on them, not on her—"I have something to say to you. I had meant to leave it for a little while, until after—after the funeral, you know. But now I can see there is going to be a disturbance, and an all-round fire of unpleasant questions, and a skeleton-hunt, and Heaven knows what besides. So I had better speak to you first. I want you to let me take my uncle's place to you, Deldee. Of course

you can't look up to me and respect me as you
did him ; but that doesn't matter ; we can get
on very well without that. Whatever I have
done, and however I have behaved to other
people, you will always be able to depend upon
me just as if I were—as if I were your father,
in fact. No, don't laugh!" said he earnestly,
as she uttered a little hysterical sound, in
which there was not much merriment. "A
man may be a very good father, you know,
even when he has been by no means without
reproach in—in other respects; so I don't see
why you shouldn't be—be my daughter. Yes,
I know it sounds funny ; but I must be something to you, Deldee," he went on, his voice
growing fuller, more tender ; "and—and if—
if everything had been altogether different, why
then—why then, of course, it wouldn't have
been the same, and we might have come to—
why, come to other arrangements perhaps.
But, as it is, I have thought it over, and this
seems the only feasible plan. Of course you
won't call me 'papa'"—and they both began
incoherently laughing, with tears in their eyes
—"because—because, of course, it wouldn't do.

But you will come and live here with my aunts,
and—and you won't find me much in the way
—I shall generally be out. And you can be
married from here, when I have found you a
nice trustworthy husband. But we can take
our time about that."

He stopped at last, and found, on looking
at her, that Geraldine was staring at him blankly,
with moist eyes. His suggested arrangement
took her breath away.

"You are not serious?"

"Yes, I am. Why not? Look here—it is
of no use for you to say you are not coming,
for you are to come—do you hear? There can
be nothing against it; my aunts want com-
panionship."

"Not mine," interrupted Geraldine, shaking
her head decidedly.

"Yes, they do," said he obstinately. "They
are dull, lonely. And I am dull and lonely;
I want you," he declared with a burst of yearning affection in his voice. "I—oh, Deldee,
don't say you won't come!"

She shook from head to foot as he put his
hands upon hers, and looked down into her face·

with pleading eyes her own dared not meet. She warded off his nearer approach to her, and said, speaking very fast—

"I tell you, Sir James—James it is impossible. Hear what the rest say; I know they will say it is impossible. And don't, don't, don't turn away like that, as if you were angry with me. You must know I don't want to be unkind."

"Then you promise to come, if they all agree to it?" said he, turning eagerly and abruptly.

"Oh, I don't know! They won't agree, I'm sure. They will say you are mad."

"Very well. Come and see."

He drew her hand through his arm, and led her off to the drawing-room, walking very quickly and without speaking. The lamp had been brought in, and round it the two elderly ladies and the Vicar were sitting. James, who seemed restless and excited, pulled the bell very sharply when the greetings were over, and gave the unaccustomed order—

"Another lamp, and some candles—lots of candles!" Then he turned to his aunts. "I

can't bear this gloom; it oppresses me. You
don't mind a little more light, do you?"

Eleanor looked horror-struck. More candles! And at such a time as this! It was
an outrage on decency as well as a criminal
extravagance. Elizabeth assented to the order
rather stiffly. Both the guests felt relieved,
however, when Johnson came in with another
lamp, followed by a maid bearing candles.

"That is better!" exclaimed James; and
then he violated precedent again by bringing
up an unused ottoman from the other end of
the room, placing Geraldine on it, and throwing
himself down upon it beside her.

It was a bad beginning, denoting contempt
for the sacred rights of custom, easy familiarity
with the opposite sex, and unhealthy discontent
with existing arrangements. But it was but
the prelude to something far worse; for, as
soon as he was seated, he began, with his
eyes still on Geraldine, who tried in vain to
prevent his speaking—

"My dear aunts, I have a proposal to make
to you, and I take the opportunity of making
it in Mr. Bamber's presence, because I feel

sure that he will support me. You all know
that Geraldine, the little sister I found so
romantically and brought here nineteen years
ago, was my uncle's adopted daughter." There
was a movement on the part of both the elder
ladies ; but neither of them spoke. " You all
know how fond he was of her, and "—here
he lowered his voice—"that she was his last
thought on his death-bed."

"James !" interrupted his younger aunt, in
a stifled voice.

He put up his hand authoritatively.

" Let me go on, aunt, and we will come to
the discussion presently. You know perhaps
—you certainly do, Aunt Elizabeth—that I
have looked already for my uncle's will, and
can find none but one he made twenty years
ago. We all have reason to think that he
made another just before he died ; but, as he
was at that time under the influence of design-
ing persons, who disappeared as soon as I
surprised them by turning up, we are not
likely to hear of that one again. Now it was
certainly not his intention to leave the person
he loved best in all the world unprovided for."

Geraldine tried to interrupt him ; but he kept her silent. "And it seems to me that the best way in which we can carry out his wishes with regard to her is by adopting her in our turn and bringing her here to live with us, whether," he added, as she shook her head decidedly, " she likes it or not."

There was a minute's complete silence. A thunderbolt had fallen upon them all, not in his proposal, but in the suggestion which accompanied it—"to live with us." Then he proposed to remain here among them. Was he then free to do so ? It was an awkward moment for them all. The Vicar came to the rescue.

" Your plan is not a new one, James," he observed, "though perhaps I am the only person here who has heard of it before. On the very day before his illness, Sir Charles told me that it was his intention to bring Miss Geraldine to the Hall, having learnt, I fancy, that Miss Gretton, her protectress for so many years, is anxious to leave Copsley and enter what the High Church people call a retreat."

James's eyes were sparkling with triumph ;

and he took both the girl's hands affectionately in his.

"You hear that, Deldee; you hear that, Aunt Elizabeth! My uncle wished it, and his wishes are sacred to us all now."

Elizabeth was trembling with anger, and for a moment dared not trust herself to speak. For this artful James had cleverly planned his attack so that the presence of the Vicar should shield his favourite, this odious interloper, who had wormed herself into his affection as she had done into his uncle's, from the effects of her just indignation. After only a few instants' pause, Mr. Bamber spoke again.

"But, my dear James," he began, with diffidence which his rattling voice was unable to express, "you must excuse me for broaching this extremely delicate subject; but, as it has to be done sooner or later, it may as well be got over at once. I would suggest that there are certain difficulties, of which you must yourself be fully aware, in the way of your making any arrangements for settling the family affairs. As an old friend, whom you have all known for any number of years, your aunts appealed to me to ask you to take them a little more into your confidence than you have hitherto done, before you have the inevitable interviews with the executor, who is—so Elizabeth tells me—Admiral Stanhope."

"Confidence!" echoed James, his face suddenly lowering. "What about?"

There was another most awkward silence, during which nobody could keep quite still.

"Well, then, not to beat about the bush any longer, how did you—did you manage to get here, in fact? In the pleasure we all felt at seeing you among us again, we—we—none of us—could rush into details directly, nor could you, of course! But you can see yourself, my dear boy, that it makes all the difference in the world—that it is a point which your relatives have a right to have settled, in fact."

"What on earth do you mean?" inquired James, in a low voice. "I don't understand you."

"Well, then, if you force me to speak out, how did you get out of prison?"

"Prison!" echoed James, quietly.

"Yes, Dartmoor, I believe it was. Were

you let out, or—or have you—well—er—
escaped ? ”

James looked at him steadily, as he crossed
and recrossed his legs and tapped the table by
which he was sitting, and shifted his coat-
collar as he was in the habit of doing his gown.

“ I have never been in prison,” he replied
very calmly.

There was instantly a great commotion in
the room, though nobody spoke except poor
Eleanor, who began to pray aloud in a quaver-
ing voice for forgiveness for his perjured soul.

“ My dear James,” said the Vicar very
gravely, “ think again.”

“ If I think till I’m blue in the face, I
can’t find a suitable reply to such nonsense ! ”
retorted the young man angrily. “ I—I can’t
think what has come over you all. I beg your
pardon, Mr. Bamber ; but really such questions
would try any one’s temper. Deldee,” he
added, turning to her with sudden excitement,
“ did you ever hear this story before ? ”

She turned a white face towards him,
whispering in an agony of trembling hope—

“ Oh, James, isn’t it true, then ? ”

" True ? No, of course it is not true ! Where on earth did you all get hold of it ? So this is the meaning of—— Good Heaven ! "

He started up from the ottoman and leant against the mantelpiece, with his head in his hands. They all looked at him mutely, not knowing what to make of his behaviour—all but Elizabeth, who got up and left the room as the butler appeared at the door.

" Then, if this is not true, how do you account for your long absence without ever sending your friends any intimation of your whereabouts? " asked the Vicar.

" When I left Waringham, it was with the intention of severing all connection with a place which I had hated since my boyhood, and a family who had hated me, and who were bent upon forcing me into a profession which I "—he remembered his interlocutor, and changed his sentence—" for which I was unfitted."

" And you have been—— "

" Everywhere. To—to—to the Cape for the greater part of the time."

But that fatal hesitation made the Vicar look graver still.

"And you mean to say that you deny— absolutely deny that you were ever in prison ?"

"Most emphatically I deny it!"

"I am afraid you will find that difficult to prove, as two persons whom we know well, to begin with, saw you in prison."

"And who are those two persons ?"

"Sir Charles's Dublin solicitor, Mr. Massey, a man whose evidence is unimpeachable, and Mr. Lindley Fielding."

"Lindley Fielding!" almost shouted James, contemptuously. "Is that the evidence you have to go upon ?"

"It is not all of it, James," broke in Elizabeth, coldly. She had come into the room while they were talking, holding in her hand some newspaper cuttings and a letter. A sort of detestable exultation over this man who had wished to thrust Geraldine upon them made her blue eyes glitter brightly. She glanced over the papers in her hands, and, deliberately selecting one printed extract, give it to him to read.

He took it and held it close to one of the candles on the mantelpiece. He was breathing heavily, and he had to pass his hand across his

eyes before he could read. It was an account
of the trial, a short one—being only an Irish
murder, the newspapers had not given it much
space—but clear, giving all the names. Geraldine crouched on the ottoman, unable to look at
him. He laughed a hoarse laugh that grated
on the ear, and said, in a choking voice—

"It—it is a mistake; it is too absurd.
Inquire—inquire at Dartmoor, or—or wherever
it is, and you will find that your—your felon
James Otway is safely caged."

"Unfortunately no, James," responded
Elizabeth, very quietly. "I sent Martha to Goldborough this afternoon, to the Post-Office, to see
if a letter I expected from Mr. Massey, in answer
to one of mine, had arrived. She has just
brought it. I will read to you the paragraph
which concerns you." She unfolded the letter
and read—

"It is quite true that James Otway made
his escape from Dartmoor five weeks ago. I
only heard of it two days since, or I should have
written to you. He is supposed by the police
to have left for Australia; and, as he has kept
out of their hands so long, I should think, with

proper precautions, he ought now to be safe."

"Would you like to read it yourself?" She was handing the letter to her nephew, when, with a gasp and a gurgling sound in his throat, he staggered forward and fell in a fit.

The Vicar led Geraldine quickly from the room, and insisted, in spite of her prayers, upon leading her off at once to the Vicarage. She sat, like one stunned, almost unable to answer Mr. Bamber's gentle and kind speeches, until the little Norfolk cart was ready, and Reginald helped her into it to drive her back to Copsley.

Just as they were starting, and her straining eyes were striving to pierce the evening mist that hung about the trees of Waringham Park, she whispered huskily—

"Oh, stop, stop, one moment, I implore you!"

Reginald reined in the pony, and in another moment the figure she had dimly seen came up to them. It was James, panting, haggard, ghastly.

"Deldee, Deldee, for Heaven's sake, say you don't believe it!"

"Oh, James, no, I don't—I don't!"

The poor fellow seized her hand and clung to it in a paroxysm of gratitude.

"Thank you, thank you! God bless you!" he cried hoarsely. "Come again. Let me see you again."

"I will come to-morrow," she whispered tenderly close to his ear.

He seemed only half to understand the words; but the tone of her voice comforted him; and, as Reginald touched the pony lightly with the whip, to put an end to this distressing interview, James pressed her hand to his hot, dry lips, with a look which wrung her very soul, and staggered back without another word, as she was driven away from his sight quickly in the dusk. A spasm of terror seized Geraldine, as she turned to her companion.

"What will he do? What will he do?" she cried wildly.

"Oh, he will be all right to-morrow! The whole business has been clumsily managed, and I don't wonder it upset him," replied Reginald, soothingly.

But a leaden fear fell on the girl's heart that she would never see James Otway again.

CHAPTER IV.

REGINALD BAMBER was a man whose even
temperament placed him above the reach of
petty stings of jealousy, and, moreover, it was
quite out of the question that he should for a
moment entertain such a feeling as envy for
an escaped convict who inaugurated his freedom
by drunkenness, and who had then the audacity
to deny that he had ever been in prison at all.
But, from what he could see of Geraldine's
face, as he drove her quickly in the dusk of
the closing evening from Waringham towards
Copsley, the girl was evidently so entirely
absorbed in anxiety for that most unworthy
object of it that a natural uneasiness arose in
his mind ; and he said, in his soft voice—

"You are far too good-natured, Miss
Lindley. I don't know any man who is worthy

of all the kind compassion you are bestowing upon one who certainly does not deserve a tithe of it."

"That is not a very Christian sentiment," she answered, her voice trembling. "And yesterday you accused me of being too severe."

"Yesterday I had reason to hope that you were," he expostulated gently. "Yesterday Otway had not put himself outside the pale of sympathy by what I can really call by no other term than a deliberate and audacious falsehood."

"How do you know it is not true?" she asked hotly.

He saw by this wild question that she was not in a fit state of mind to be talked to as a reasoning being, so he answered indulgently—

"Of course, of course—how can we know? We must wait and see."

But she, detecting mild compassion for her imbecility in his tone, said, with a strong effort to be calm and collected—

"Mr. Bamber, what would you say if I were to tell you that, in spite of appearances, I believe Sir James's word."

This was too much for a man's patience. Reginald answered quietly, " I should be obliged to say, Miss Lindley, that it was a very remarkable instance of the amiable weakness which puts a woman's judgment, however naturally keen, at the mercy of her affections."

" It is no question of the affections," she said quietly, but in a tumult of inward rage at being accused of an " amiable weakness." " It is a matter of weighing the evidence for and against the truth of a statement."

" But, unfortunately, all the evidence is on one side," urged Reginald, still with perfect sweetness, though he began to feel mild annoyance at her obstinacy. " It all goes to show that there cannot possibly be a particle of truth in Otway's denial of his having been in prison."

" A James Otway was put in prison, we know, but not necessarily this James Otway."

" That was settled at the time. He was actually seen in prison by a man in whom Sir Charles had the greatest confidence, a man of unimpeachable character — Mr. Massey, his solicitor in Dublin."

" But there was another person who visited

the prison, whose evidence, you will admit, is not so unimpeachable—Mr. Fielding."

" Of course his visit counts for nothing."

" I don't think it does. Mr. Fielding is Sir James's greatest enemy ; he himself says so, and he is very clever and cunning, as every one says."

" But he is not clever enough to impose upon a man so well acquainted with his character as Mr. Massey is. Besides, Mr. Massey had nothing to do with him ; he went himself to the prison and saw Otway."

" But did Mr. Massey know James by sight ? "

" Yes. Sir Charles sent his nephew over to Dublin on purpose to see this lawyer about some business of his ; James duly called at the office, and it was then that he disappeared ; nothing more was heard of him until his name appeared in the papers as that of one of six men charged with the murder of the farmer Hughes." Geraldine shuddered. " That was within fifteen months of his disappearance ; therefore there could be no difficulty about recognizing him."

" I believe Mr. Fielding had something to
do with it," persisted Geraldine impulsively.

" 'Something to do with it' is rather a
vague charge. He cannot, however, have had
anything to do with putting Otway into prison,
because I happen to know that he was in
London when the account of the murder
appeared in the papers, and that he had been
in town for some time. It was just before I
first went out to America, and I was staying
with an uncle of mine in Cromwell Road making
preparations for my journey, and I used
frequently to meet Mr. Fielding, who was, as
usual, in difficulties, and trying to induce his
relatives to help him to start some financial
speculation or other."

Geraldine listened very attentively. Reginald Bamber was an excellent authority for
facts, and especially for facts concerning the
Otway family, for Sir Charles had been in the
habit of confiding in the Vicar, who, in all
matters of difficulty, relied much upon the
judgment of his steady, serious son.

" Then it could not have been Mr. Fielding
who got some man to take the name of James

Otway, and then got him into prison?" suggested Geraldine foolishly.

But Reginald did not laugh. Her remark was plaintive in its lack of reason. He explained gently—

"That would have done no good to him or harm to anybody else, while the real James Otway was alive and free to come forward and prove his identity whenever he chose. As it happens, it was I who pointed out the paragraph about the Irish murder to Mr. Fielding. I was going up to the Temple station by the Underground Railway, and he got into the same carriage. When I first saw the name, it did not occur to me for the moment that it could be Sir Charles's nephew, and I showed the paper to Mr. Fielding. He was astonished, unmistakably astonished, and, after looking at the announcement for a few moments, he said, with some show of triumph—

"'Then I'm not the only scamp in the family; I've kept out of the papers, at any rate!'

"And he said at the time that he should go and see him if he could, out of curiosity as much as compassion."

"Then why does James say that Mr. Fielding is his greatest enemy?" asked Geraldine, much puzzled.

"Does he say that? I am afraid poor Otway is in the mood to think all mankind his enemies. I think that nervous depressed state he is in is the surest possible sign that he has been recently in some great trouble, the effects of which are upon him still."

"Yes; but we don't know what that trouble is. To-morrow I will ask him to tell me."

"To-morrow!" echoed Reginald, in a marked tone.

"Yes, yes! Did you not hear him ask me to come to Waringham to-morrow?"

"Yes."

"And would he have asked me to come and see him if he did not intend to be there?"

"Certainly not! The question is whether he will be able to carry out his intention of remaining."

"Why not?"

"If your supposition is correct, and he has really nothing to fear from the police, then, of course, there is no reason against it. But if

my view of his position is the right one, then
there is the strongest possible reason why he
should make his stay as short as he can."

"Then if he is still at the Hall to-morrow,
you will believe that he is innocent?" said
she in triumph.

"I won't pledge myself to that; but, of
course, the longer he stays the stronger is the
argument—the sole argument—that he has
nothing to fear in staying. But, if you value
his liberty, I warn you earnestly not to put him
to the test of inducing him to dare the police.
A man might easily be rash for the sake of
standing well in your eyes; but I know you
would not like poor Otway to pay such a
penalty as he would have to pay if he were
caught."

"I believe that he has no reason to fear
being caught," she persisted staunchly, "and
I will do my best to induce him to prove it
to-morrow."

In spite of all her loyalty, her voice
trembled a little on that last word, for she
remembered the fancy she had had, while
standing with James under the cedar trees

that afternoon, that she could see the figure
of a man lurking in the black shadow cast by
the branches upon the high wall which shut
out the stable-yard from the garden. If the
police were indeed already watching the house!
Suddenly her faith gave way to deepest anxiety,
and she turned imploringly to her companion.

"Oh, Mr. Bamber," she whispered, "if he
really has done it, he is brave—too brave!
I warned him this afternoon ; but he took no
notice of what I said. Perhaps at this moment
they have caught him, for I saw a man—at
least I think I did—crouching hidden near the
Hall to-day. Oh, what shall I do—what can
I do ? "

"You can do nothing now," he answered
gently, pitying her distress. " But, as soon as
I get back, I will go straight to the Hall, and
see if anything is going on there, and, if I get
a chance of speaking to Otway, I will do so."

She thanked him warmly, and was almost
silent, wrapped in her fears, for the remainder
of the drive ; but she gave him an eloquent
look as she bade him good-bye, to remind
him of his promise.

To do him justice, the reminder was needless. He drove back as quickly as he could to Waringham, gave the cart into the charge of the Vicarage coachman, who was a valuable retainer, not too haughty to make himself useful in the house and garden, and walked up to the Hall. It occurred to him to inquire at the lodge if any one had been through that evening.

" No, sir, barrin' two undertaker's men, sir, and Mr. Fielding—leastways, think it was him, sir; but he passed rather quick."

Reginald went straight up to the house, and asked if he could see Sir James.

" Sir James has gone to bed, sir."

It was only nine o'clock; but having heard from his father the Vicar that James had had a fit of some kind that afternoon on being shown the letter from Mr. Massey which made his own denial of his crime useless, Reginald was not surprised that the young man had retired early. However, he remarked, as if rather surprised—

" He keeps very early hours then ? "

" It is exceptional, sir. Sir James has not

been very well to-day," answered Johnson discreetly.

" Has the doctor been to see him ? Wasn't it the doctor who came a short time ago ? "

" No, sir ; no one has been since the Vicar and Miss Geraldine left."

" Oh, well, I'll call again in the morning and see how he is."

Something was going on—that was evident. The question was, Where ? It is an awkward undertaking to prowl round a neighbour's house in the character of a volunteer detective ; but it was too critical a moment for the calmest of men to stand upon ceremony. Reginald had noticed a light in the library, and the curious fact that one of the shutters had either been only partially closed or else had been partially opened since the closing. This fact had been easy to discover by the perpendicular stream of light that came through the white blind. When Johnson shut the door, Reginald, remembering this, went straight down the drive between the flower-beds, and passed out into the park, to put possible watchers off their guard, and then passed round over the grass among the trees to another entrance to the garden, leading through the grass-walk and the rose-corner to the principal entrance again. He tried, as he made his way under the trees of the park, to see whether his disappearance had encouraged any lurking figures to come forth; but he was by that time, being rather short-sighted, too far off to distinguish anything at the library window. When, however, he made his way cautiously round to the principal entrance again, and thence to the corner of the house, where, concealed behind an ornamental fir tree, he had a good view of the façade of the building, his patience was rewarded not only by the sight of three men crouching under the library window, one of whom appeared to be looking in, but by hearing some of their words.

For the first few minutes he could make out nothing intelligible, nor could he understand how a man could see through a linen blind. Growing bold as he became accustomed to his position and felt his security, Reginald pressed himself so closely into the fir tree as to be within a few yards of the three men, for the library

was the first room on this side of the house.
And then he recognized the man nearest to him—
one of the two who were crouching down and
not looking in—by voice and figure as Lindley
Fielding.   And, as he kept quite still and held
his breath, he heard the man farthest from him—
the second crouching down—say—

" How long were you warder while he was
there ? "

" Two years, or thereabouts."

" Then you couldn't make a mistake ? "

" Not exactly."

" Then you are satisfied ? " whispered
Lindley.

" Quite, sir."

" Then your work is done ; and yours "—
to the other man—" is all before you."

" Yes, sir ; but it is pretty plain sailing
now."

" Then come away where there is less risk
of being seen."

Lindley raised himself softly, carefully hid
the traces of his visit by digging up, with a
bit of stick, the mould his feet had pressed
down, and, stepping on to the path, made his

way towards the back of the house, followed by
his two companions. As soon as they had
turned the corner, and were out of sight,
Reginald stepped quickly to the library-window.
A slit recently made with a pen-knife in the
white blind, and enlarged just enough to give
a good view for one eye into the room showed
the means by which the warder had recognized
the escaped convict. The window was not
fastened, and this fact suggested to Reginald
that the means of observation had been cleverly
made from the outside. He looked in and
saw that, as he had expected, James Otway was
the only occupant of the room. He had
evidently been writing at the bureau, for he was
standing before it, fastening down an envelope;
and Reginald's eyes, calmly observant even at
that exciting moment, noticed from the rapidity
with which he snatched up a pen and scrawled
something on it, that the letter was not intended
to go by the post. And the next guess he made
was the name written on it, for James pressed
his lips to it as he strode hurriedly across the
room to the door. The few moments' pause
which Reginald had made was not the result of

curiosity, but of consternation at the young man's appearance and manner, of consequent hesitation as to the best way of making the startling announcement the latter had to hear. For James's face was flushed, his eyes were heavy, his hands trembled as they held the pen ; he was evidently the prey of some strong excitement. Reginald wondered whether he had been forestalled in his warning ; his momentary delay lost him his chance of speaking, for James left the room so quickly that his friend's sharp tap at the window was lost in the opening and shutting of the door.

"James !" he called ; but it was too late. He went back quickly to the entrance, rang the bell, and, while waiting, tore off the blank half-sheet of a letter he found in one of his pockets, and wrote upon it, in such French as came first into his head—

"Je viens de voir trois hommes accroupis près de la fenêtre de la bibliothèque, occupés à épier vos mouvements par moyen d'un trou dans le store. L'un d'eux était votre cousin vaurien. Je ne sais si cela doit vous inquiéter, mais puisque la circonstance est un peu hors du

commun, je trouve mieux de vous en faire part.
Ils ont disparu, mais ils ne se sont pas éloignés,
car d'après ce que je les ai entendu dire, ils
sont allés se cacher dans un autre endroit près
de la maison. Ils ignorent absolument qu'on
les ait aperçus, car j'étais en cachette. Si je
puis vous être utile à quelque chose, vous savez
bien que vous pouvez me commander. Je vais
fumer un cigare dans le parc avant de rentrer
chez moi, ainsi vous saurez où me trouver en
cas que vous ayez besoin de moi.

" R. B."

He was still engaged in writing this with a
pencil, by the light of the hall-lamp, when
Johnson opened the door.

" Will you give this to Sir James immediately, please, Johnson ? " said he impressively to the old servant.

" Yes, sir. I will certainly do so, if I can
see Sir James," answered the butler gravely.

These unorthodox interruptions to the
peacefulness of his evening hours rather annoyed
him.

" Your master has not yet gone to bed, I

know. You are an old friend of the family,
Johnson; and, as you value the peace and
safety of its members, don't fail to deliver this
at once."

As he said these words in a very low voice,
a creaking door was heard to open inside the
house. Johnson, instantly mollified by the well-
judged speech, promised to take the note to his
master, and Reginald retired into the park,
keeping watch on the house while he smoked
a cigar. As he sauntered down the drive for
about the sixth time, preferring, with his
habitual prudence, the gravel to the wet grass,
he heard the sound of a gate opening near the
house, and a noise of wheels and hoofs. He
turned and quickened his pace towards the
house; before he got very near, he heard James
Otway's voice say "All right," and, just as the
phaeton turned the corner of the house and
came in sight, Reginald saw a man's figure
crossing the garden quickly towards it from the
other end of the house. It was a mail phaeton,
and the hood was half-up, so that its occupants
could not be distinctly seen; the horses were
whipped up sharply at that moment, and the

pursuing figure, altering his course, made straight for the lodge. But Reginald guessed his object, and, throwing away his cigar, turned and ran in the same direction. He was not a particularly good runner, being indolent and without much staying power; but he was lightly built, long of limb, and had a good start of the other man. He reached the gates a hundred yards ahead of his competitor, unfastened them, panting, and flung them wide, just in time for the phaeton to dash through, while James, who was driving, said, "Thanks, old fellow, God bless you!" as the man in pursuit ran up just too late.

"Confound you!" he angrily exclaimed. " Who was that?"

Reginald made no answer, but turned to saunter back towards the Vicarage just as the lodge-keeper came sleepily out to see what was the matter. A moment after, however, the man, whom Reginald then recognized as the one who had looked through the library-window, and whom he had understood to be a warder of the prison where James had been confined, came up and, touching his hat very civilly, said—

"I beg your pardon, sir. I am sure no gentleman of your stamp would willingly impede an officer of the law in the execution of his duty."

"I don't know," said Reginald, thoughtfully, "when it is a question of saving another gentleman of my stamp from being impeded in the execution of his."

"Would you oblige me, sir, by telling me the name of the gentleman who drove out just now?"

"Upon my word I didn't see him."

"But you know who it was, sir."

"Well, and if so——"

"Then I should be much obliged if you would tell me his name. You see, he is gone, so no harm could happen to him, even if harm were intended."

"I am sorry I don't feel justified in obliging you."

"Thank you, sir. May I trouble you for your name and address?"

"My name is Bamber; I am staying at the Vicarage here."

"Thank you, sir. Good night, sir!"

" Good night ! "

Reginald returned home, sincerely glad to have been the means of helping his imprudent and unlucky friend to evade the hand of justice, but good-naturedly sorry for the bitter disappointment his guilty flight would cause to poor Geraldine. With this latter feeling, however, was mingled a little natural satisfaction at the confirmation of his own prediction and at the providential removal from her neighbourhood of a man whose society was almost contamination for a being like her.

Unfortunately, the being herself would not look at the matter in a proper light. She cried herself to sleep that night over the ne'er-do-weel's well-deserved misfortunes, and was on thorns next day until the afternoon, when, escorted by Miss Gretton's most trusted servant, who combined the duties of ladies'-maid and upper-housemaid, she started by train for Goldborough, where she took a cab to Waringham. She had been wily enough not only to refrain from defending James from Miss Gretton's attacks, but to join in disparaging him in favour of Reginald Bamber. For all that, she sat well

back in the cab that she might not have to delay
her arrival at the Hall in order to stop and
speak to Reginald, when she caught sight of
him walking slowly along the road just outside
the park-gates; but he was not so near-sighted
as to fail to see her; and, while her heart beat
fast and her eyes sparkled with impatience, he
stopped the cab and came up to the window.
She was too much excited by thoughts of some
one else to notice that he did not look quite so
calmly superior to human emotions as usual.

"You are going up to the Hall, Miss Lindley?" he asked, when she had answered his
greetings rather shortly.

"Yes; I — I want to see whether Miss
Eleanor is any better."

"I am afraid you won't find her very well
to-day." He paused. "I am afraid you will
find them all in some anxiety."

She looked at him with suddenly awakened
attention, the colour dying out of her face.
Reginald looked down at his boots, as he added,
in a lower voice—

"It is all right; everybody is well and safe;
but—James—— "

" What! Make haste, please ! "

" Nothing; only — James went away last night."

She said nothing for a few moments, and he did not look at her; but he heard her breath coming in short quick gasps.

"Went away! How?" she whispered, at last.

" Oh, he is all right; he went by himself! " he answered reassuringly; and, looking at last into her wistful, anxious eyes, he felt for a moment that he actually envied the escaped convict James Otway. " I—I didn't mean to alarm you ; he is quite safe by this time—— "

" By this time!" she echoed, in anxious inquiry.

" Yes. There were some men here last night who tried to stop him ; and I think one was a detective. And you were right about Mr. Fielding ; it was he who brought them."

A sudden fire woke in the girl's sad eyes.

" How did you find out all this ? " she asked, after a pause.

"Did you think I should forget my promise?" he asked reproachfully. " I came straight back here last night, as I told you I should do. I

saw and heard the men, wrote a note to warn
James, waited in the park till he came out, and
opened the gates for the phaeton just in time
for him to drive through before one of the men
came up to stop him.   Haven't I kept my word
to you ? "

" Yes," said she, in a choking voice ; " thank
you ? "

He would rather have seen her less pro-
foundly grateful ; but it was something to feel
the warm pressure of her hand, to see the soft
light in her eyes, even for this service rendered
to his—no, no, not rival, but—well, this contemptible *protégé* of hers !

Their whispered conversation was over, and
the cab was driving slowly through the park.
Geraldine did not cry ; but she sat very still,
and asked the maid to draw up the windows,
with a sudden feeling that it had grown very
cold.   She had for an instant debated within
herself whether she should not now turn back,
instead of exposing herself uselessly to the
taunts and unkindness of Miss Elizabeth, or
even to the possibility of that lady's having
given orders that admittance should be denied

to her. But, for the first time, now that there was no one at the Hall to protect her from the younger Miss Otway's savage insolence, Geraldine felt her fear melt away; and the resolve to find out all she could about James's departure caused her to conquer every outward trace of nervousness before she arrived at the house.

Johnson's usual stolidity gave way when he saw her. Alarm, relief, anxiety, showed themselves by turns in his face, when, having ordered that the cab should wait, she asked for Miss Otway. As soon as he had conducted her far enough across the hall to be out of hearing of the maid, he stopped, and saying, in a low voice—

"Sir James left Waringham last night, ma'am, and intrusted me with this letter for you, and told me particularly not to let it out of my hands to any one but you," he handed her a letter addressed simply to "Miss Geraldine" on a salver which he had taken from the hall-table as he passed.

So great an apprehension did the butler entertain of Miss Elizabeth's rummaging propensity that he had not slept the night before

until he had locked Sir James's letter safely in
the plate-chest.   Geraldine tore it open at once,
and Johnson retreated respectfully into the
inner hall, from the safe shelter of which he,
however, being quite as deeply concerned in
the affairs of the Otways as the young lady
herself could be, watched her as she read it ;
and he saw : first, that she was very deeply
moved by it, though she stood quite still and
uttered no sound ; and, secondly, that the
emotions the letter produced were not all pain-
ful ones, though her eyes were full of tears long
before she had read to the end.   The letter
was as follows :

"My Dear Geraldine,
        "I doubt whether you will be able
to make out what little sense this note contains ; perhaps you will laugh at the silly
confession I dare not make in any other
manner.   I love you, Deldee, and for love of
you I am going away to-night—where, I do
not know.   Don't trouble your kind heart
about me, for I am only leaving a place I
hate for the sake of a woman whose love

I may not win. I have no wife, Deldee, for
the woman I married has left me ; but she is
still alive and —— "

There was more still to read when the
drawing-room door opened and Elizabeth came
out. If Geraldine had not been so much excited and absorbed by the letter in her hands,
she would have been more surprised by the
changed manner of the lady, who, after a glance
at the letter, held out her hands most cordially,
and said, with her bright, artificial smile—

"Come in, come in, my dear Geraldine.
You will have to let me call you Geraldine now.
Your arrival could not possibly have been more
opportune."

She led the girl, who slipped her precious
letter quickly into her pocket, into the drawing-
room, where, with a little cry she could not
repress, Geraldine recognized James's would-be
betrayer, Lindley Fielding. He was sitting beside Eleanor, whom the sorrow and excitement
of the past few days seemed to have withered
up and rendered more like a witch than ever.

"That man !" she whispered, in too low

a voice for the exclamation to reach his ears.
" He says he is your father," said Elizabeth,
in a voice just as low, detaining the girl for a
moment.

" I will never believe it."

" Well, my dear child, I happen to have it
in my power to prove that it is not true; therefore you need not be afraid of him."

Geraldine was beginning to feel bewildered
by this unexpected kindness; but she was led
forward without time for reflection.   Just as
Lindley rose and came towards them with out-
stretched hands and a smile of effusive affection
upon his face, Elizabeth stepped in front of the
girl and said—

" One moment, Lindley.   Before you give
this young lady the hearty welcome which I see
you have prepared for her, it will be better for
her to know in what character she is to be
received among us."

" Certainly," assented Lindley, beaming with
paternal tenderness.

" We have decided, Geraldine," continued
she, turning to the perplexed girl and taking
her hand, "that the best way in which we can

carry out the wishes both of our poor brother,
Sir Charles, and our unfortunate nephew, Sir
James, is by requesting you to make your home
with us." Involuntarily Geraldine shrank back.
"You cannot refuse," continued Elizabeth, "for
circumstances have come to our knowledge
which make your stay at Waringham a duty
as well as a right." Lindley was looking
satisfied, but rather surprised. "Mr. Fielding,
at the time of my late brother's illness, made
certain statements about you which, for some
reason or other, he, on the unexpected appearance of our nephew James, denied, and which
he still denies." Lindley looked less satisfied
and more surprised. "His motive I have not
yet discovered. But, in the mean time, I have
made inquiries about his first statement, and
have found, to my surprise, I confess, that it
was true."

Lindley fairly started.

"Elizabeth, take care what you are saying!
Do you know——"

"I know that from the moment there is no
longer any mystery, any family secret in your
hands, your interference in our affairs must be

at an end, Lindley," she went on, with cold, slow triumph. " So, with many thanks to you for your obliging offer to take this young lady off our hands in the character of your daughter, I beg to inform you that your offer of service is needless, and that Miss Geraldine Otway will reside for the future in the house of her late guardian, under the care of my sister Eleanor and myself, who, in pursuance of our brother's wish, adopt her as our niece."

It was a blow to Lindley, for this bold stroke had indeed cut the ground from under his feet. Geraldine living at the Hall as his daughter, and in the pride of his secret he had stipulated that she should live there, would have given him right of entry, social standing, and more solid benefits in the way of perquisites; so that he stood confounded, admiring, in spite of himself, the bold manner in which Elizabeth had cast aside prejudice in order to outwit him.

Having resolved upon a daring course, Elizabeth pursued it worthily, and ended by telling Geraldine that, as soon as possible after the funeral, she should expect the girl to come

and take up her residence at the Hall. As
she wisely rose, to leave the girl a little time
for reflection on this bewildering communica-
tion, Lindley, who had recovered from his consternation, approached his cousin in his usual
airy manner, and said, in a low voice with a
smile which had no irresistible charm for her—

"So you think it is check-mate, my fair
cousin? But you ought to know better. You
have met my opening move well; but the
game is only just begun. Keep your eyes on
the board, that you may make a fair fight of it,
as, with your spirit, I am sure you would like
to do; but the end will be all the same."

"I dare say you think that sort of talk very
clever, Lindley; but I confess I am not good at
it myself; so I will tell you in plain English
that you are quite at liberty, as far as I am
concerned, to play what games you please,"
said Elizabeth, without taking the trouble to
lower her voice as she left the room.

CHAPTER V.

No sooner had his cousin left the drawing-room than Lindley Fielding, forsaking Eleanor and her moaning affection, crossed to where Geraldine sat staring out at the oaks in the park. The sight of the middle-aged Adonis who had first disturbed her peace in Copsley churchyard, whose ill-considered announcement had killed her guardian, who was James's enemy, and whom she feared as she had never feared a human being before, was extremely distasteful to her. But he approached her so respectfully, apologized for obtruding upon her so courteously, that it was impossible to meet his well-managed advances with a rebuff.

"It has been my misfortune, Miss Geraldine," he began gravely, "to be associated in

your mind with several distressing circumstances;
nevertheless, I hope you will remember that it
was through my feint of assuming the happy
position of father to you that my cousin
Elizabeth was induced to fulfil her duty towards
you. No, no, I want no thanks ; no one ever
thinks of thanking me. There is hardly a
member of the family whom I have not served
at one time or another, and you see how they
treat me ! "

" I am afraid your services towards them
must sometimes have been misunderstood, Mr.
Fielding."

" Perhaps so ; but is that my fault ? " he
asked, with much meekness.

" I don't know. Do you think James Otway
has reason to feel grateful to you ? "

" Most assuredly he has ; and the time will
come—I acknowledge that it has not come yet
—when he will confess that he owes more to me
than any one in this world."

" He doesn't by any means take that view
of his obligations to you now," said she rather
drily.

" What does he charge me with ? " asked

Lindley, in a tone of patient resignation to calumny, but with a glance of keen inquiry.

" He speaks of you as his worst enemy ; and, indeed, if it be true, as I have been told, that you brought the police here last night, I can't think his opinion of your services to him too highly coloured," replied Geraldine, with rising passion in her voice.

Lindley, who had been unable to repress all show of consternation at her mention of the police, quickly recovered from his astonishment and heaved a deep sigh, perhaps to gain a little time for thought.

" My usual luck ! " he exclaimed at last, with a shrug. " You have only heard one-half of the story. When I found that the police were after him, I came with them, in order to delay their movements while I found means of warning James to escape."

' " It was you, then, Mr. Fielding, who sent word to him that the police were upon him ? "

" No," said he frankly, seeing by her tone that it would be unwise to assume the credit of his kinsman's escape. " By some means or

other he got wind of their arrival before I
could send word to him ; and I rejoiced at this,
for the fact of his having taken a most unreasonable prejudice against me would perhaps
have prevented his believing a message from
me."

"You admit that he is prejudiced against
you ?"

"And I add that the prejudice is a most
unjust one. You shall judge for yourself." He
watched her narrowly as he continued, speaking
slowly and with great precision. "When James
was committed to prison, five years and a half
ago, charged, with five others, with the murder
of Hughes, the farmer, I went all the way from
London to see him, being the only one of his
relatives who took any trouble about him—I
confess with some curiosity to see whether it
really was my relative, James Otway of
Waringham, who was in this sorry plight ; but
I went at the same time prepared to do all in
my power for him, should this prove to be the
case. But he, doubtless having heard nothing
but abuse of me all his life from my kind
relatives, took it into his head that I had come

to exult over him—imagine a poor devil like me
exulting over anybody!—and assailed me with
a volley of hard words, which I bore pretty well,
as I am used to them."

"And you mean to say this is the sole
ground of his mistrust of you?"

"It is, I assure you."

"Had you never seen him before?"

"Not since he was a boy, when I used to
tip him with the half-crowns which were never
very plentiful with me."

"What a very strange antipathy!"

"Strange indeed, Miss Geraldine; but I
intend to overcome it."

"I am afraid you will not find that easy."

"I agree with you; but to me the difficulty
of an undertaking constitutes its charm. Now
the difficulty of mine can scarcely be exagge-
rated; for not only have I set myself the task
of overcoming James Otway's mistrust of me,
but I have determined to earn his gratitude by
enabling him to make a fresh start in life—out
of the country, of course."

Geraldine started.

"Never to come back to England!" she

murmured. " It would be as bad as being in prison."

" I don't think James would agree with you in that, hard as it of course is to be cut off for ever from—one's relatives. One consolation I can however give you, Miss Geraldine—he is the sort of man to accommodate himself easily to change of circumstances, to pluck what pleasure comes to hand, to make himself happy wherever wine is cheap and—well, I need not mention the other condition."

"Yes, that is just the impression he gave me," said Geraldine coolly.

Lindley, who was impressionable, and whose strength lay in his power of exciting himself, began to find this girl who could think for herself irritating and depressing; and, with a feeling that if he remained any longer in her society he might spoil the impression he had made, which was not wholly unsatisfactory, he soon found means to break up the *tête-à-tête*, and to rejoin the less attractive but more sympathetic Eleanor, who, from the farther end of the long room, had furtively watched them and wondered what they were talking about.

Then Geraldine left the room in search of Elizabeth. She wanted to exchange a few more words with that lady on the subject of the astonishing revelation of that afternoon, and then to go back to Copsley and to pour out the strange tale to Miss Gretton ; she wanted, above all, to look once more at the dear dead face of her father. She went from the outer to the inner hall and called " Johnson ! " in the hope of his being about. He appeared from the dining-room, and approached her rather mysteriously, with a glance round at the various doors and a glance up the staircase. Then he produced a well-worn man's morocco pocket-book, which, in perfect silence, he put into her hand, with a look of some triumph.

" What is this ? " she asked, surprised.

Johnson glanced around and above again before he answered her in the oracular tone which the imperfectly educated delight to assume at a time of excitement.

" There have been many strange things going on here lately, ma'am, things that we must wait the Lord's time to clear up. Mrs. Symes, I have reason to think, knows more than anybody; but she is close, as perhaps is best under the circumstances. Mrs. Symes gave this to me, ma'am; she picked it up in my poor dear master's room, and she said to me—'Give this to Miss Geraldine; she has the best right.' She gave it to me not ten minutes ago, ma'am, when she heard you were here."

"Who is Mrs. Symes?" asked Geraldine, looking at the pocket-book, which contained some letters, with an uneasy feeling of mystery upon her. "Is it that dreadful-looking old woman?" she began, and then checked herself.

"Yes, ma'am; she is the housekeeper."

Geraldine was inclined to fancy that the weird, gray-faced woman had cast some spell upon the pocket-book which rendered it a thing with which it were better to have nothing to do. Besides, whoever was the owner of it, it was clearly not she; but it then occurred to her that this Mrs. Symes, who had sat by Sir Charles's death-bed, and who was reported to know so much, doubtless knew that she was his daughter, and, in any case, must have good reasons for this course; so, after examining the outside of the pocket-book with much hesitation, she was proceeding to open it with strangely reluctant fingers, when the butler, who had watched her movements of uncertainty and surprise without a word, softly turned the handle of the dining-room door and held it open for her.

"Will you step in here, Miss Geraldine? Mrs. Symes said you had better look over it in private."

The girl's curiosity was now fully roused. She went in, holding the pocket-book tightly against her, as she glanced rather timidly round the great, dark room, which she had never been in before, and up at the gloomy oil-paintings of vacuous-looking dead Otways that stared down out of heavy, dingy gold frames from the walls. She drew a heavy chair to one end of the wilderness of table, and sat down with her back to the lofty conservatory into which the room opened, a dreary place big enough for the tropical trees at the Botanical Gardens, which it would have been better to leave empty than to garnish with a couple of indiarubber plants, a row of sickly camellias, and a meagre show of

geraniums and other plants to be bedded out
later in the season.

Geraldine was in a few moments far too
deeply absorbed to notice either plants or
pictures, for the contents of the pocket-book, as
she turned them out, one by one, and placed
them on the table, were a series of enigmas to
which she had no clue. First came half a dozen
letters, addressed in different hands to " Henry
Hammond, Esquire, 103, Duncan Street,
Brompton." These had all been sent through
the post and opened. She ascertained this,
and placed them, without further investigation,
in a pile together. Next came a cutting from
a newspaper giving an account of a street row,
with no names, but with the hint that " It is
pretty well known who the principal delinquents
were, and the parties are advised to settle their
little domestic difficulties indoors another time."
From the literary style Geraldine gathered that
the paper from which this was cut did not take
high rank; from the advertisements on the
other side, and the curious Dutch names, she
learnt that the paper was published in one of
the Colonies. The next thing she took out was

a photograph. It was the portrait of a girl in an ill-fitting dress of the style of a few years before, a girl so young and so pretty, even when judged through the medium of this somewhat inartistic reproduction, that one could forgive the want of taste which had led her to towzle her hair too much in front and to curl too much behind, and to deck her round throat with a collar made of "tatting," fastened by a brooch and a bow of ribbon, and finished off by a couple of cheap necklaces. This photograph had been taken at Holloway. On the back was written, with a fine pen, in a scratchy, sprawling woman's hand, "To dearest Harry, with Ada's love." On the memorandum-leaves of the pocket-book were entries in a man's handwriting, probably that of H. Hammond, the owner. Some of the leaves had been torn out, leaving others loose; one fluttered to the ground unnoticed by her. She glanced at some of the entries; they were merely a man's odd jottings, sometimes in the form of an attempt at a diary, sometimes stray memoranda. The entries afforded her little information; on one page, for example, were the following—

" 18*th*. Dined with Russell. Don't like his wife ; he advised me to turn over a new leaf. What leaf ?

" 19*th*. Popped my watch. This won't do !

" 21*st*. Went to Abbey ; heard Canon—— Could have preached better myself. So many well-turned sentences in so many minutes.

" 22*nd*. Saw a body fished out by London Bridge. Looked beastly. Thames wouldn't do —should strike out in—— "

Here the page ended. The next entries were fragments of medical prescriptions, the title of a work on poisons, and a chemist's address in a poor part of London.

The nature of the fragments of diary interested Geraldine enough to make her wonder who the writer could have been, how the book could have got into Sir Charles's room, and why it should have been sent by the housekeeper to her. Nothing seemed clearer than that it had not belonged to her father ; the handwriting was a pencil scrawl unfamiliar to her. She was proceeding in some perplexity to open one of the letters, when a hand was suddenly laid upon the whole pile, at the same moment that

the pocket-book was quickly and neatly trans-
ferred from her keeping to that of Lindley
Fielding, who stood by her with some anxiety
in his eyes, but with his mouth expanded into
his favourite bland smile.

"Miss Geraldine—Miss Geraldine, I did not
expect to find you tampering with other people's
letters!" said he, with playfulness which was
rather forced.

"And you may be sure I should not do so
without authority for such an action," she
answered with dignity. "I must beg you to
return me the pocket-book and the letters at
once."

"That would be reversing the natural order
of things," he responded, with that persistent
smile which began to irritate her as much as it
did Elizabeth. "This pocket-book is not yours,
but mine."

"Yours! Your name is not Hammond!"

"When I say it is mine, I mean that I have
more right to it than you. Mr. Hammond is
my most intimate friend. May I beg, in my
turn, that you will give me the letter you were
reading?"

When Lindley's hand had so unexpectedly
swooped down upon her, Geraldine had instinctively kept out of his reach the letter
she had just taken up, and she still held it
firmly.

"If you can give me some proof that what
you say is true, you shall have the letter," said
she, after a pause.

But Lindley smiled on. Placing his spoils
carefully in one of his pockets, he took from
another one a handful of letters and papers,
and, selecting one letter, showed her the signa-
ture at the end, "H. Hammond." Then he
replaced it in his pocket in triumph. Reluctantly Geraldine gave up the letter she held
and it was not until it was safely in his fingers
that it occurred to her to say—

"But you did not show me that that letter
signed 'Hammond' was addressed to you."

Lindley laughed outright—quite easily now.

"Oh, where have you learnt to be so sceptical — you, who are still in the age of innocence?"

"I learnt it, Mr. Fielding, in Copsley churchyard," she replied coldly.

Having gained his object, he had retreated a little way, and was criticizing the old pictures airily through his eye-glass. As Geraldine was rising from her chair, she caught sight of one leaf of the diary on the ground at her feet, and she did not scruple to defraud Mr. Hammond and his most intimate friend by slipping it into her pocket as she, with great airs of dignity, left the room. Standing at the foot of the staircase opposite was the gaunt housekeeper, who had evidently been waiting for her, as she stepped forward at a pace rather quicker than her usual stately march.

"You got the pocket-book, ma'am?" she asked, in a low voice.

"Yes; Johnson gave it to me. Whose was it?"

The nervous old woman, who inspired Geraldine with absolute fear by the drawn look of horror which seemed petrified upon her withered face, glanced round her before she answered, in a croaking whisper which made the girl feel quite cold—

"I found it by Sir Charles's bedside, ma'am; and I think it was dropped there by——"

She had no time to ask any more questions, for at that moment a light suddenly fell upon the sibyl-like figure in front of her, and Geraldine saw the old face contract with terror which infected herself. Turning sharply, she saw that the dining-room door had been opened by Lindley, who was standing with his eyes fixed upon the housekeeper with a warning, almost menacing expression. The old woman's lean hand falteringly sought the support of the oaken banisters, while her frightened eyes never left his face.

" What is that you are saying, Mrs. Symes?" he asked suavely.

But she stood as if paralyzed, without answering him.

" Why, we shall have to get the doctor to come and prescribe for you, Mrs. Symes!" he continued slowly, though still with much urbanity. " You look quite ill, I declare?"

She made a rapid eager gesture of dissent, at least it was rapid for her.

" No? Not ill?" he went on. " Well, if you wish to continue in good health, I think you cannot do better than follow the prescrip

tion Doctor Ledbury gave you. He did give
you one, did he not ? "

" Yes, sir," she murmured at last.

" Well, keep to that ; you can't do better."

And Lindley, almost afraid of the effect his
presence evidently had on the trembling old
woman, went into the outer hall towards the
drawing-room ; but he was stopped in his
leisurely stroll by Elizabeth, who said, with a
smile as sweet as his own—

" I have ordered the phaeton, Lindley, to
take you to the station, as I knew you would
want to catch the express back to town."

He was taken aback, only for a moment—
then, showing all his fine teeth in a grin of rage
and annoyance which had no effect upon his
cousin, he said—

" I won't pretend to misunderstand you—
you turn me out ! I warn you that, when my
turn comes—and it will come very soon—I
shall not feel bound to show much chivalry for a
lady who takes the family affairs into her hands
in so high-handed and masculine a fashion ! "

" Ah, I hear the carriage ! I hope you won't
have a cold journey."

"Thank you; it will not seem cold after my reception here. I shall have the pleasure, Elizabeth, of seeing you again."

She gave him her cold finger-tips, still smiling; but, as he drove away, her face contracted and her eyes grew anxious. She had defeated the enemy and had forced him to retreat; but he had forces in reserve, and there might be a desperate conflict before her yet.

CHAPTER VI.

Two months passed quietly away after Sir Charles Otway's death, during which time Lindley Fielding gave no sign. The affairs of the late baronet were still in course of settlement, and at the same time inquiries concerning the story of Geraldine's birth were being pursued, without, however, much success. But as both Eleanor and Elizabeth, to everybody's surprise, announced their belief in it, and formally recognized the young girl as their niece, she was constrained to leave the care of Miss Gretton for the far less sympathetic guardianship of the ladies at Waringham Hall. A reason for Elizabeth's change of front soon appeared. It was discovered that Sir Charles had been a good deal better off than people had supposed—the rigid economy of a score of

years had had its effect ; and a sum of several
thousand pounds, well invested, which he had
privately set apart and left in trust to Mr.
Massey as a provision for the girl who was
now said to be his daughter, was found to have
been the result of his frugality. What cautious
steps could be taken to find out where James
Otway had sought refuge were taken in vain—
being a convict, he could not of course claim
the property ; but means would have been
forthcoming to help him to settle somewhere
abroad, had he made his future course known
before leaving Waringham. But he had disappeared as suddenly as he had come, leaving
no trace, and with no farewell, except the letter
to Geraldine, which the girl mentioned to no one.

She never spoke about him, except to deny
her Aunt Elizabeth's suggestion that it was his
absence which made her so grave. For the
buoyancy of her youthful spirit she seemed to
have left behind her at Copsley. Whether it
was the sadness consequent upon her father's
death, or the depressing atmosphere of the bare
old house, or the unsympathetic society of her
aunts, one of whom, however, found uncon-

fessed comfort in her presence—the warm and
balmy days of June found her still melancholy,
still silent, finding her only pleasure out of
doors, not under the trees of the park or among
the bright flower-beds which broke up the
smooth lawn in front of the house, but in the
old garden, shut in by the two iron gates in
the shadowy rose-corner where James had
gathered the long-since-withered sprig of Scotch
rose which she looked at by stealth so often in
her own room, or else sauntering down the
grass-walk, as she had sauntered with him,
or standing, as she had stood with him, beside
the great square pond among the trees which
now held leafy branches out over it, looking
at the green, smooth weed which was gradually
making its way over the whole surface of black,
stagnant water, and at the slimy, water-logged
boat silently decaying, as it stood moored to
its rotten post at the farther end. And she
stood and watched the water and the gnats
that swarmed over it, and the hanging birches
and the thick tangle of trees and brushwood
that hemmed it in, not in listless mournfulness,
but with her head on fire with wild plans for

bringing the man she persisted in considering the rightful owner of the Hall back again.

She was forcing her way through the trees, on her way back from the pond one afternoon, her face still lighted up with her fancies, and her lips softly uttering the words of a song, when she came face to face with Reginald Bamber, and the song died away. She liked Reginald; he was very kind and very handsome, and he had helped James to escape; but the ungrateful girl could not forget that it was he who had prophesied that her favourite would have to escape, and the fact that his prophecy had come true only increased his offence. She knew at a glance what he had come for to-day; though she had never been wooed before, she knew that it was in the character of a wooer prepared to take the final plunge that he stood before her, with his habitual calmness a little bit shaken and an unmistakable air of having made up his mind to look his best that day, or die in the attempt.

They were both confused; and she, talking fast, led the way towards the house; but of course he wouldn't go.

" You have come from the old pond, haven't you ? " he asked. " I should like to look at it again ; I haven't seen it since I was a boy."

" There is nothing to see," said she, stopping reluctantly as he held back the branches for her to pass through—" nothing but a horrid, unhealthy pool covered with duckweed."

" We used to think it a lovely place when we were boys, though," he remarked, gaining his point by persistency. " James and I used to catch tadpoles in it and put them in bottles, and we used to pull Tip, his terrier, across on a raft ; and we used to have wrestling-matches in the boat, which wasn't water-tight even then, I remember."

" It is very deep, isn't it ? "

" I don't know. They always say that of old ponds. 'Deep enough to drown a man in some parts.' You are not meditating suicide, I hope ? "

" No—o," said Geraldine, thoughtfully, as if she had not quite made up her mind.

" A pond," continued Reginald, evidently growing nervous, " is such a paltry place to drown one's self in—the Atlantic would be better; I am going to cross the Atlantic in a few weeks."

"Are you?" she asked quickly. "And are you glad to be going back again?"

"Glad—and sorry. Under—under some circumstances I should be wholly glad."

But she was not in the least interested to know what those circumstances were, and nothing would induce her to meet the eloquent look which would have told her—what she knew already. But he was going through with the matter now.

"It is not that I mind leaving England," he went on; "it is the—the people in it—at least, some of them—one of them."

"Poor Mrs. Bamber will miss you dreadfully, of course——"

"My mother has my father and my two brothers. I think you know it is not my mother I meant. Don't pretend to misunderstand me," said he, nervously pulling the leaves off a birch tree behind her. "I have wanted to speak to you for a long time, and I have never found the—the courage till to-day.

Don't tell me you don't know what I mean;
I think you must. They say every woman
knows when a man cares for her, and I think
you can't help knowing I have cared for you—
ever since I first met you. You do know it,
don't you, Geraldine?"

"Oh, I'm so sorry! I did try to prevent
you," she cried, looking up, with a face full of
remorse and misery. "I did know what you
meant, and I did try to stop you; but you
would go on."

Then there was a pause, during which each,
without looking at the other, could hear the
quick breathing that told of agitation. At last
Reginald spoke very gently and sweetly.

"Why won't you have me, Geraldine?"

"Oh, don't put it like that!" said she
ingenuously. "It isn't that at all. It is—it is,
on the contrary, that you are so much too good
for me. Yes, yes, it is true, I do really mean
it; not that I am particularly wicked, but that
you are so particularly good."

"But if that were true, as I am sorry to say
it is not, wouldn't that be considered rather an
advantage in a husband?"

"Yes, of course ; but it would give you too great an advantage over me."

"But," suggested he very sweetly, a little amused in spite of himself, "if I am so very good, don't you think my influence might convert you from your wicked ways in time ? "

"But I don't want it to ! " she broke out, laughing hysterically.

If Reginald had been able to retain his usual calm prudence in the face of this defeat, they might have parted on the most friendly terms ; but his head was just a trifle heated by the excitement, his heart slightly bitter over the disappointment, and his vanity a good deal hurt.

"Will you let me try my fortune with you again, Miss Otway, if, in the mean time, I endeavour to conform myself more to your taste ? "

" I don't understand you."

" If I were to leave my friends for months not knowing what had become of me, and let their first tidings of me come through the police-news, or if I were to be seen in a state of intoxication—— "

" Then certainly I should have a much

higher opinion of your good taste and good
feeling than I have at this moment, Mr.
Bamber," she interrupted. She had become
as white as death to her very lips, and the fire in
her dark eyes seemed for the moment to have
gone out. "For in the instances you mention
you would be doing harm only to yourself,
while your words just now have given, as
you meant them to give, the deepest pain to
a girl who has certainly never wished to harm
you."

"I should be doing harm only to myself,
you say. Surely murder harms some one
besides the murderer?"

"James Otway is not a murderer," she cried,
with sudden passion, the light flashing swiftly
back into her eyes and the colour to her face.

"Then he has been much belied."

"He has. But, with Heaven's help, his
character will be cleared some day."

"Indeed I hope it may. In the mean time,
he is much to be envied."

Her enthusiasm she suddenly reined in, and,
after another short pause, she said tranquilly—

"You think I am in love with him, and that

it is on his account that I refused you. Neither supposition is correct. It was through the boy James Otway that I was not brought up as a farmhouse drudge; it was through the man James Otway that I was able to see my father on his death-bed. I am indebted to him, therefore, for all the happiness I have ever enjoyed; and, if he were never to be seen sober, and if murder were his favourite occupation, my debt to him would remain the same."

"Then, of course, you forgive a great deal?"

"I could do so; but I believe there is no need. At least I believe that he is accused of a crime he never committed. As for his faults, that is another matter; I see them as plainly as you can do, and they are even more repellent to me, a woman, than they can be to you, a man. You mistake entirely the nature of my feelings for James Otway. If I must speak out clearly to explain away the offence my words seem to have given you, I will tell you that, though I hope and believe that he will prove his innocence, if he were to return here a free and stainless man, I could not marry him."

" If he is innocent, why did he run away ? "

" He went to seek proofs of his innocence ; he left a letter to tell me so," she replied, blushing.

Reginald looked sceptical.

" Then why doesn't he come back ? "

He had touched the sensitive nerve, and her face grew troubled in spite of herself. James Otway had been away two months, but had made no sign. She turned away impatiently.

" Don't be angry with me," said he. " I will believe anything you like about it ; I will let you persuade me that he has some good reason for staying away."

She turned upon him quickly.

" You talk as if my trust were quite a childish thing that one could forgive and excuse in a silly girl, but which it was out of the question for a man to consider seriously. But it is a man who encourages me in my belief, a man whose judgment even you would allow to be worthy of consideration."

Reginald looked surprised and incredulous.

" Captain Morrison says he has heard many stranger stories, and he says we ought to take

some steps for finding James out, or we may
lose sight of him again altogether, just as we
did six years ago.   It was not a crime which
made him hide himself then, remember."

"Then, if he has gone away merely from a
dislike to staying at home, it seems a waste of
time to try to drag him back against his will,
doesn't it?   Why is Captain Morrison so
anxious for him to come back ?   Does he know
Otway ? "

"Oh, no !   It is only an abstract question of
right with him ; but it interests him, and he is
always ready to talk about it.   In fact, it is the
only subject he is ready to talk about—you
know how silent he generally is."

"Yes," said Reginald, thoughtfully.

This Captain Morrison was a lately arrived
resident in the neighbourhood, a gentleman
about whom nothing was known except that he
was reported to be "very rich," who had taken
a small furnished house about half a mile from
the Hall, which he had now occupied for two or
three weeks.   He had excited Reginald's
jealous attention by losing no time in making
the acquaintance of the Misses Otway, and

young Mr. Bamber was therefore on the alert
to look with suspicion upon the slightest
peculiarity in the conduct of his possible rival.
He could condescend to use that word in connection with Captain Morrison, who was, it
could not be denied, a quiet, well-bred gentleman
of inoffensive manners, bigoted in his opinions
like most soldiers, but with sense enough not to
obtrude them on any one. Indeed, his excessive
reticence and reserve was the one charge which
even Reginald could at present find to bring
against him. The young man, however, at
once fastened upon this remark of Geraldine's
with the determination to try to find out what
this special interest of the stranger in James
Otway and his fortunes might mean. That it
meant something he, of course, at once decided;
that it meant something which might offend
Geraldine he was ready to hope. For the
rebuff he had met with that afternoon had by no
means been severe enough to make him give up
hope, especially since that frank declaration of
hers that she would not in any circumstances
marry James Otway. He had indeed done her
that justice in his thoughts; but he was glad to

have the belief confirmed by her own lips. In spite of himself, he rather liked her the more for her obstinate defence of the man whom she now called her cousin, and he managed to intimate this to her as a peace-offering before they went into the house and the *tête-à-tête* broke up.

On the whole, he felt, as he left the Hall, very little like a rejected lover, a state of feeling not due entirely to temperament, but partly also to the fact that he had kept the currents of emotion and passion so well under control that Geraldine had been entirely unstirred by them, and had been able to refuse the devotion of a life with hardly more agitation than she would have shown in declining an invitation to dance. " Rather a cold woman !" he thought to himself, as he walked through the park towards the lodge and noticed how very full the foliage of the oaks was already ; but, on the whole, it was a fault which he could tolerate as well as any. If it made a girl difficult to win, it would make her easy to keep. His hopes of ultimate success were not much disturbed by his meeting Captain Morrison riding up to the house, although it was on horseback that the little officer looked his best, for the latter could not ride into the drawing-room at the Hall and woo Geraldine from the vantage-ground of a remarkably firm seat on the back of a chestnut thoroughbred, which he had used as a charger ; no, he would have to dismount and disclose the lamentable fact that his height was only five feet two inches, or rather less than that of Geraldine herself.

Nature had been rather unkind to the captain ; for surmounting that mean and insignificant figure was a head which, on a taller man, would have commanded a good deal of admiring attention. It was finely shaped, the curly, dark hair grew well round a broad, intellectual forehead ; the features of his olive-skinned face were clear cut, and the large, deep-set brown eyes and sensitive mouth suggested strong capabilities both of resolution and passion. It was an interesting as well as a striking face ; the more closely it was examined, the better it was known, the more it suggested both of good and evil.

Miss Elizabeth received him very graciously. She had not disdained to make some inquiries about the stability of his fortune, and they had been answered in the most satisfactory manner. An old friend of the family, Admiral Stanhope, had answered for his position and character; and, as the stranger began to show admiration for Geraldine, her aunt congratulated herself already upon her wisdom in adopting a girl who lost so little time in proving herself a credit to the family. It was rather remarkable, considering how reserved the man was, how quickly he had got sufficiently into Geraldine's confidence for her to speak to him quite freely upon the subject of the missing James Otway; perhaps it was the evident fact that he listened with real interest, and not merely with lover-like attention, which made her speak to him on this matter so openly. For they were never long en *tête-à-tête* without touching upon the subject, though the girl herself could seldom tell what had led to it; his interest in the matter, which, if she had cared more about his attention, it would have occurred to her to think was even deeper than that he felt for herself, caused her no surprise; she was too much absorbed by it to wonder at the attraction the subject had even for a stranger.

On this afternoon, as soon as he had an opportunity of speaking to her privately, as he handed her a cup of tea, he asked—

" Have you any tidings yet ? "

" No," she said mournfully.

" Do you think he can have got into bad hands ? "

" What do you mean ? "

" Has he any enemies ? "

" Oh, yes ! " she answered faintly, with a spasm of terrible fear at her heart.

" Have you no means of finding out anything about their movements either ? "

The girl did not answer for a moment ; the question had raised a good suggestion. She still had the card Lindley Fielding had given her in the churchyard.

" I don't know—perhaps," she said, at last hurriedly, in a low voice ; but she would say no further word to him on the subject, though a light of interest came at once into his eyes as she spoke.

Happy in the belief that he was making

love to her niece, Elizabeth was ready to give
them plenty of opportunities for conversation ;
but, from the moment of that suggestion, Geraldine became absent and unintelligent. Something, too, in Captain Morrison's eager attention
had made her shrink back from further confidence, she scarcely knew why ; no distant and
delicate offer of his help in her search, should
she make any, no fresh assurance of his sympathy, could induce her to utter another word
on the subject. From that day she avoided it
with him, for no distinct reason ; and, seeing
this change, he had the tact to let the matter
drop.

But his suggestion burned into the girl's
brain nevertheless ; she pondered it by herself,
it grew the stronger for being confided to no
one ; and at last she resolved, with fast-beating
heart and a hundred nervous girlish fears, to
act upon it. Miss Gretton was staying in
London with some relatives of hers, before her
final settlement into the semi-religious com-
munity in which she wished to pass the remainder of her days. Geraldine wrote to her,
asking if she might come and spend a week

with her before her final separation from the
world.   The invitation obtained, the girl com-
municated it to her aunts, who rather unwillingly
agreed to let her go.   Eleanor sincerely missed
her gentle attentions; Elizabeth sincerely wished
not to lose her control over the girl and her
money.   In the last days of the London season,
therefore, Geraldine, attended by an encumbrance her aunts would not let her dispense
with, in the shape of a silly maid who could not
be trusted out of sight with anything of more
value than a newspaper, arrived in Russell
Square at the boarding-house kept by a married
niece of Miss Gretton's.

The girl's plan was formed, and, on the first
day after her arrival in town, she put it in force.
On the pretext of having some commissions to
execute for her aunts, she chose the afternoon,
when her old instructress was lying down, to
send for a hansom and start off in it.   To her
extreme annoyance, Miss Gretton put her head
out of her room at the last moment and insisted
upon the encumbrance, Susan, going too.   What
was to be done with the girl ?   To take her all
the way was out of the question, for she would

make the most impossible of confidants. To leave her at a pastrycook's was not to be thought of, as she would have time to eat up everything in the shop and then run out, frightened, in search of her mistress. The British Museum would alarm her by its dulness, the South Kensington was out of the way.

"Would you like to see the Tower of London, Susan?" she asked persuasively.

It was the one earthly delight she most craved. So they drove to the Tower; and Geraldine, after strictly warning the girl not to leave the building till she came for her, gave the cabman Lindley's address in the city, and drove off in high excitement. She had never been in London, except on her way to and from France; on those two occasions she had spent a few hours only in it with her guardian. The city was quite new to her, and a place of wonders and terrors; the hurrying crowds of men made her think some startling event had happened somewhere, and the way in which they ran under the very noses of the horses made her journey one long effort to keep herself from crying out. At last the hansom

stopped before the entrance to a narrow paved
court; and the driver said, "It's up there,
ma'am!" So she got out, and made her way
timidly up the dingy court, among the hurrying
throng of men, who puzzled her a good deal;
she could not make out whether or not they
were gentlemen. They stared at her very
attentively, but made way for her as courteously
as the hurry they all seemed to be in would
permit. And one tall, fair, young man, who
wore his hat on the back of his head and
blushed as he spoke to her, raised his hat and
asked her if he could help her to find the
number she wanted; but she did not like to
accept his offer, so he blushed again, raised his
hat, and hurried along as before. Soon she
was sorry she had declined, for she wandered
about, unable to find No. 4, for all the numbers
seemed to be covered up by printed names,
and nobody else offered to help her. She
thought this crowd of busy men very unfeel-
ing, and would have been much surprised to
hear that it was want of courage which prevented them from helping her. At last she
found a policeman, and begged him to show

her which was No. 4; but he stared blankly
at the houses round him and accompanied her a
little way up the court, and then said there
wasn't a No. 4; and her heart was sinking,
when a gentleman, who overheard this, pointed
out the house to her, and the policeman said,
"Oh, ah, yes, to be sure!" and took her shilling
and went away.

But now a new difficulty arose; for among
the printed names which covered the posts of
the entrance there was no name of Fielding.
But, after a careful search, she found that the
newest-looking title of all was the "Anglo-
European Financial Development Association"
in very big letters, that its office was on the
ground-floor, and that the manager was "Mr.
Field"—in very small letters. And she thought
she would try that. So she found her way to
the second door on the ground-floor, where the
same inscription stared her in the face on the
ground-glass upper half of a door. She could
hear a shuffling sound inside, and dimly see
a figure bobbing about, for her first knock
was not heard. At her second louder knock
the noise ceased, and the figure disappeared; a

few moments later the door was opened by a
thin boy with rough hair, who looked very
warm, and who asked her to come in. She
came into a very dark and dingy room without
much furniture, opening into another, which
looked darker still.

" Is Mr. Fielding here ? " asked Geraldine,
doubtfully.

" He has left the office for to-day, miss. Is
there anything I can do for you ? I am Mr.
Fielding's private secretary," he said, with an
important air.

" Oh, no, I don't think so, thank you ! Can
you tell me where he is gone to ? "

" He has gone home, miss. He will not be
here again till to-morrow morning. If it is any
matter of business, I shall be happy to give you
any information."

She thought him an insufferably affected
little boy—he could not have been more than
thirteen, and she asked coldly—

" Can you give me Mr. Fielding's private
address ? "

" Very sorry, miss ; but it's against the rules
of the—of the association."

Geraldine could understand this rule in an association of which Lindley was the head, little as she knew of business. She wondered whether the private secretary was above bribery.

" I am giving you a great deal of trouble," she murmured, "and—er—I assure you you need not think Mr. Fielding would mind your giving his address to me;" and she produced half-a-sovereign from her purse.

The poor private secretary's dignity collapsed at once; he had never seen so much money at one time since he had served under the association.

"It's not for any harm to him, is it? Honour bright ? "

" No ; I assure you it is not."

" And—would you mind—could you—not say anything—Oh, well, never mind that."

He took the half-sovereign with eager eyes, and gave her the address, offering to write it down ; but she said she would remember it. He then took his hat to escort her to the cab, and on her suggesting that he had better not, lest any one should call in his absence, he

volunteered the statement that there wouldn't
be anybody—to matter.   So she got back more
easily than she had come, and the still radiant
private secretary gave the cabman the direction
" 59, Langton Street, Porchester Place."

Within half an hour, Geraldine found herself
at the door of a house at the West-end with a
card bearing the word " Apartments " over the
door, and, on inquiring for Mr. Fielding, a
dirty servant told her Mr. Fielding was not in,
but was expected, and would she wait ?   Geraldine accepted the invitation, and was shown
by the servant up to the second floor.

" What name shall I say, ma'am ? " and, to
the surprise of Geraldine, on being told, she
opened a door and announced " Miss Lindley ! "

And Geraldine found herself in the presence
of a well-dressed lady, with a bright, pretty,
surprised young face.   She almost started, for,
in spite of a great improvement in style, she
recognized in the pretty little dark head, with
hair cropped short like a boy's, the towzled and
ringleted head of the girl whose portrait she
had found in the strange pocket-book—" To
Harry, with Ada's love."

CHAPTER VII.

THE discovery that the pretty little woman before her was the original of the photograph she had found in the pocket-book of the unknown " H. Hammond " startled Geraldine Lindley so much that her momentary embarrassment affected the cause of it, who bowed and held out a pretty little hand rather nervously.

" My husband won't be long—in fact, I'm expecting him every minute ; he ought to be back by this time," said she. " Won't you please sit down ? "

She was rather awkward and shy, and her accent was not very refined ; but she had such a pretty face and such a trim, slender figure, and the inquiring way in which her long, gray eyes looked up under their curling, black lashes was so irresistibly winning that Geraldine was quite charmed by her, and thought what a pity it was such a sweet woman should be thrown away on a man like Lindley. It occurred to her that this meeting was fortunate, and that she was far more likely to get the information she wanted from this chatterbox, who was prattling away very fast already, apparently glad to get somebody to talk to, than from her more cunning husband. Mrs. Fielding prepared the way herself by undisguised curiosity concerning the object of the lady's visit.

"Do you want to see my husband very particularly? Because I can't quite tell how long he'll be, you know," she said naïvely.

"Yes, I want to see him very much; but, if you think he is not likely to be here soon, I had better call again to-morrow."

"No, don't go; I'm so dull, and so glad to see anybody," said Mrs. Fielding quite eagerly. "Is it anything I can help you in?"

Geraldine hesitated.

"You are very kind. I have been adopted by some relatives of Mr. Fielding's."

"Oh, yes, I know who you are!" interrupted the other promptly.

"We—we are all very anxious at Waring-ham to know whether a nephew of my adopted aunts, who is at present away from home, is well. Mr. Fielding expressed an interest in him, and I came to ask if he could relieve our anxiety about him."

She had spoken thus freely because, at the first allusion to James her hearer's manner had become suddenly so mysterious that it was evident she knew something about him. Mrs. Fielding nodded several times, with pursed-up lips, and then said, in a loud whisper—

"Sir J. O.? Well, I think I can tell you all you want to know about him."

"Oh, can you? Is he safe?" asked Geraldine, eagerly.

"Yes, he's safe enough, I believe, at present ; but he's got nearly to the end of his tether by this time, and I should think he'd have to run for it again very soon."

"Run for it! Where is he, then ?"

"Ah, I mustn't tell you that! At least, to tell you the truth, I don't know his address ; but he was here last night."

"Here! James here !"

"Sh-sh, yes! I don't believe they think I know half so much as I do ; but, if Lindley will keep me shut up with hardly anybody to speak to, of course I'm bound to amuse myself the best way I can, you know. It's only natural, isn't it ? "

"But they are enemies! They are not friends !"

"Oh, yes, they are! I know there was a row some time ago ; but they've got over that, and I know there's a talk of J. O. going abroad again, if they get too close upon his track."

"Going abroad again, do you say ? "

"Why, yes! Didn't you know he'd been abroad ? "

"Yes ; but not lately."

"Well, he's only been back a week ; if you don't call that ' lately ' —— "

"Only a week ! Where has he been then ? asked Geraldine, trying hard to appear less deeply interested then she really felt.

"Oh, they've been all over the place— France, Spain, Italy ; they've done a lot in nine weeks !"

"Has Mr. Fielding been with him then ? "

"My husband!" said she, with a burst of laughter. "No; he would have been rather *de trop*, I should think."

Geraldine dared not put another question: a great fear had fallen upon her; she felt strangely agitated, and she waited, while her breath came quickly, and a fluttering, choking sensation rose to her throat from her heart, for the other to continue.

"I shouldn't have let my husband go with them if he had wanted to; he is not too much to be trusted at any time."

"How long has Sir James been married?" asked Geraldine, speaking slowly, and controlling her voice with some difficulty.

"Married! He isn't married; at least—— Oh, of course, if you like to put it like that, he was 'married' just after Sir Charles died! But it had been going on before then, you know," she added mysteriously.

"Not married?" said Geraldine, in a low voice.

"No. How can he marry her while Mr. Farquhar is alive? unless, of course, Mr. F. divorces her. But I don't expect, between

ourselves, J. O. will keep constant long enough
for that."

Geraldine rose, unable to bear more of
these revelations, made, too, in a tone and
manner that jarred upon her delicacy at every
sentence. But she stood stupidly confused,
shaken, absolutely unable to see or find her
way to the door.

"What's the matter?" cried her active
hostess, jumping up in alarm, and instantly
effacing the bad impression she had just made
by her pretty solicitude. "Oh, I see, it's my
fault—I told you too suddenly! Never mind;
sit down; let me get you a glass of wine; yes,
do! Didn't you know of it, then?" she added,
after a pause, during which Geraldine had sat
down again.

"No," said she quietly. "We had not
heard all the story."

"It's very sad, isn't it?" said Mrs. Fielding,
changing her tone with some tact, "and very
wicked, too. However, he'll have to pay for
it soon, by all accounts."

"But surely he knows the danger he is in,"
said Geraldine, quickly.

" Love makes us all blind, they say."

" And you don't know where he lives ? "

" No. He's always a rover, and he'd need to rove now."

Geraldine paid little heed to some voluble but vague comments which followed from the little chatterbox, on the wickedness of men in general and the impossibility of trusting them. Even now she resisted the conclusion that James, who had been so gentle, so sweet, so grateful for her kindness, who had sworn in the incoherent letter he had left for her that one of the motives of his sudden departure was the resolution to clear himself from the charge brought against him, could be the subject of this second story of guilt. Still clinging to her old belief that he was the victim of some conspiracy, of which Lindley Fielding was the promoter, she cast about quickly in her mind for some form of question which would be likely to lead to a clue.

" You have seen James Otway yourself ? " she asked.

" Oh, yes, lots of times ! " she answered, surprised. " I tell you he was here last night."

" Do you like him ? "

"Oh, yes! Jimmy's a nice fellow. He used to be rather glum and gloomy; but he's got over that, and is very jolly; he and I have great fun."

Geraldine listened with tightly-compressed lips. It was a convincingly likely view to be taken of James by a woman of Mrs. Fielding's level of culture. A flush of shame at her own interest in this man rose to her cheeks, and for one moment she felt inclined to retreat, satisfied that he was unworthy another thought of hers. But, even as she rose to take leave, some subtle misgiving as to the trustworthiness of the evidence against him rose again in her loyal mind: and she asked abruptly—

"Do you know a man named Hammond?"

In an instant the manner of the giddy little woman underwent a complete change. The colour left her cheeks, the smile died out of her face, the chattering lips fell into silence, as she started up with round, staring eyes fixed upon her visitor with fear and suspicion.

"Harry!" she faltered at last, in an altered voice. "Do you come from him? Where is he? What have you come to say?"

Geraldine was bewildered.

" Harry ! " she echoed unintelligently.

" Yes, Harry. Now don't pretend—— "
She stopped and stared at the other more
calmly still. " Why, she's not pretending ! "
she exclaimed at last, much puzzled. " Then
why do you ask ? Where do you come from ?
What do you mean ? " she continued, her voice
rising higher and higher in impatient, amazed
inquiry.

" I only asked if you knew a man named
Hammond ? "

The name caused the woman to start again,
and to shudder.

" Yes, of course I do," she said in a whisper.
" You know that, or you wouldn't ask. Now
tell me quickly ; what does he want—and is he
anywhere near ? "

She was in such evident terror that
Geraldine made haste to say—

" Don't be frightened. I tell you I know
nothing about him : I have heard the name,
and I want to know who he is."

" Well, don't ask me then, and don't ask
my husband, for he isn't likely to tell you much.

In fact, I don't know anybody who will, for it is a subject we're all rather shy of."

" Who is he ? "

" I—I daren't tell you. It is of no use to ask me."

" Well, why is everybody afraid of him ? Is he some very wicked person, or "—a new thought striking her—" is he some one connected with the police ? "

" I don't know anything," answered the other, fidgeting about, and then suddenly brightening as a knock and a ring were heard.

Geraldine felt that her chance had escaped her. A minute later, Lindley, having already learnt her arrival from the servant, entered the room with an expansive smile of welcome.

" What happy chance has procured us this most unexpected pleasure ? I could scarcely believe the evidence of my own ears when the maid told me who was here," said he, having already discovered by the traces of agitation in both women, that some sort of exciting interview had taken place.

" I am staying in London for a few days

with my old governess; and, having learnt
your address, I thought I would call and inquire
if you had heard anything about Sir James
Otway. You know you said you were going
to help him, Mr. Fielding."

He glanced at his wife, saw by the guilty
manner in which she avoided meeting his eyes
that she had been prattling, and by the inquiring
anxiety in the face of the other that nothing of
serious importance had leaked out.

"I have heard from him," he admitted
cautiously.

"You have done more than that, you have
seen him!" said she quickly.

He looked at his wife, whose pretty eyes
implored him not to be angry with her for her
indiscretion. Then he turned, with a smile.

"Some things you came to learn you have
already learnt, I see ; now what is left for me
to tell you ?"

Under his bland manner it was not difficult,
in a man of so emotional a temperament as
Mr. Fielding, to detect anxiety. Geraldine
hesitated. He turned to his wife.

"Now, Ade, what have you told Miss

Lindley? What is there left for me to
tell ?"

She looked at him pleadingly as she faltered
out—

" I only said that I had seen him, Sir James
Otway, lately—and—and that he had come
back—and—and had been away—and—and
Mrs. Farquhar——"

Her voice died away entirely; but her
husband, with his hand on her shoulder, took
up her speech reassuringly—

"Yes, yes, that is quite true, my dear; and
what next ?"

" Nothing else, I think," said she, brightening at once.

"Well, and what more do you wish to
know, Miss Otway ?" said he, still smiling
more urbanely than ever. "Sir James is at
present fairly out of harm's way in one sense,
though I regret to say that in another," he
continued, assuming the air of a sad and stern
moralist, "he is very far from being as safe as
we could wish to see him. This circumstance
makes it impossible, as you will understand, for
me to offer to arrange a meeting between you."

But his early and grave insistence on this point naturally woke her suspicions again.

" But you can give me his address that I may write to him ? "

Lindley looked scandalized.

" I am afraid I cannot give it to a young lady, considering the manner in which my unfortunate relative—to use no harsher term— is living."

Geraldine moved impatiently.

" Then I must hunt on my own account for his address—as I did for yours ; and I have little doubt that I shall be successful."

This timely reminder that she was a young woman of inconvenient energy impressed Lindley, who suddenly pulled out his watch, and looked at it as he evidently debated some point with himself.   Then he turned to her more coolly.

" I see, Miss Lindley, that you are unable to rise above those suspicions of my integrity which have been transmitted to you by my cardboard cousin Elizabeth," he said, with dignity.   " Since, in vindication of my own veracity, you force me to this step, I believe

that I can, if you have self-command enough
for the ordeal, give you ocular demonstration
of the truth of what we have told you."

Instinctively she shrank from the thought ;
but, as she fancied she saw that he was eager
to take advantage of this reluctance to draw
back from the offer, she summoned all her
courage and said—

"I have self-command enough ; give me
this proof, if you can."

He rose quickly, scarcely gave her time to
bid good-bye to his astonished wife, hurried
her downstairs, and into the hansom which
stood waiting for her at the door.

"King's Cross, Great Northern," he called to
the driver as he got in with her. "Drive fast."

Geraldine sat very quietly ; and her self-
contained manner did not give the least hint
to Lindley of the fear and mistrust of him
which undeniably formed part of the tumult of
strong feelings which excited her. He kept
up talk on indifferent matters, almost without
aid from her, until they came in sight of the
station, and she then perceived that he was
almost as anxious and excited as she was

herself. She had resolved that she would on
no account let herself be persuaded to enter
a train with him ; and when, after helping her
out, opening his purse and nonchalantly appealing to her with the remark that he had brought
the wrong one, he tried to hurry her into the
station, she said—

"I cannot go any farther, Mr. Fielding ;
Miss Gretton is expecting me."

His courtesy gave way at once.

"What fools women are!" he muttered
angrily. "I don't want to run away with you.
I only want you to come inside the station and
see two people who either are here already, or
will be here very soon."

He was in a state of such strong agitation
that his thick-set, muscular frame trembled as
he glanced round him with the same nervous
watchfulness that he had shown for the last
five minutes. At sight of another hansom
driving straight towards where they stood, he
left her without ceremony and hurried into the
station. As the cab stopped, however, it proved
to contain only two city men, and Lindley, who
had apparently found means of watching unseen,

came out again. Geraldine, who knew that there was no possibility of carrying her off against her will, made up her mind to follow. He led her into a waiting-room, where she sat down, while he watched the arrivals at the station through a window, and she watched him.

About ten minutes had passed, during which a few people, all of them strangers, had passed quietly in and out of the room, when Lindley crossed the floor to where she sat, without a word, but in a state of violent excitement. He touched her arm, and signed to her to come quickly to the window. They were unseen from the outside, though their own view was unimpeded. From a hansom which had just stopped a lady and gentleman had got out; the latter was paying the cabman, while the former walked slowly on towards the interior of the station. She was tall, well and handsomely dressed, of superb figure and carriage—she wore a lace veil through which it was impossible to distinguish her features; but just as surely as a certain elasticity of tread told that she was young, so surely did a certain pride in her bearing betray the fact that she was reckoned handsome. Geraldine watched her intently, without yet knowing why, while Lindley at her ear kept whispering—

" Hush, hush ! "

She did not understand, for she had not shown the least inclination to cry out. A minute later, she understood his warning. The gentleman, who had been almost hidden from view behind the lady on whom all her attention had been fixed, now hurried after his companion, and, bending towards her very solicitously, took gently from her hand the bag she was carrying, with a few words which it was impossible to hear, but whose purport was evidently very kind. Lindley Fielding, on the watch, laid his hand quickly on Geraldine's arm, with a warning whisper, as she started violently and drew a sharp breath through her parted lips.

For the gentleman was James Otway. No further doubt was possible, as she gazed steadily while he drew nearer and nearer to the window, and passed close to it, so intent upon his companion that there was no fear of his seeing any one else. She saw that the initials on the lady's dressing-bag which he was carrying were

"M. E. O."; she could hear James's voice mentioning the time at which the train was due at Enfield; she could hear that of the lady in answer. She shifted her position that she might watch them as long as possible; and then, when they had passed out of sight, she turned slowly away from the window with a rigid face and dull eyes that did not notice at first that Lindley Fielding was no longer beside her. After standing vacantly for a few moments, she collected her senses and looked round the room. Two loud-voiced women at the table were fussily counting their parcels, while their three small children, planted in a row on one of the seats, ate buns and wrangled over their relative plumminess. Nobody else was there. She hardly wondered why he had gone; it did not matter to her, she cared for nothing but to get away from this place where she had played the spy with piteous results.

Mechanically she went out, hailed a hansom, and got into it. The cabman asked her twice, "Where to, miss?" before she woke up to a clear knowledge of what she was doing. Then she suddenly remembered all the circumstances of the day, and poor Susan waiting patiently at the Tower ; she gave the direction and was just about to drive off, when Lindley Fielding hastened up. She had no thought of expressing surprise at his abrupt disappearance, but he hastened to excuse himself.

" I hope you will forgive my leaving you so suddenly, Miss Lindley," said he, with his usual silkiness, all trace of impatience and anxiety having gone from his manner. " But I had something to say to our young friend James, and of course in the circumstances I could not bring you in contact with him."

At the time he made it, she did not give this statement a second thought ; it was only later that, comparing it with the furtive manner in which he had glanced to right and left, and screened himself from view previous to James's arrival, his explanation occurred to her as an unlikely one.

She offered to drive him home ; but he said he would not trouble her, he should go by the " Underground " to Portland Road ; and, carefully avoiding any further reference to the object of her expedition, of which she now felt

ashamed, she took leave of him and drove off.
Her pride had risen in full force, and had come
to the aid of her self-possession; she stopped at
a fancy-shop to buy some wools and silks to show
Miss Gretton as the result of her journey, and,
having taken up Susan, who was incoherently
and exclamatorily delighted at the dull dissipation she had been enjoying, she drove back to
Russell Square, where Miss Gretton did indeed
discover the means by which she had got rid of
her escort, but believed that this trick was
merely a freak born of the girl's natural love
of independence.

It was not until a day or two had passed,
and the girl's watch upon herself relaxed, that
the old lady noticed a depression in her spirits,
which Geraldine accounted for by saying that
she believed the air of London did not suit
her; and she made this an excuse for returning
earlier than she had intended to Waringham,
fearing to excite still more the solicitude of her
watchful old instructress, while that of her less
affectionate guardians at the Hall would, she
knew, not be wakened so easily.

So, on a still and sultry evening in the last

days of July, she arrived at Goldborough, and, the carriage with neither of the Misses Otway in it being there to meet her, she and her simple-minded attendant were driven at funeral pace through the somewhat antiquated town, where grass grew between the uneven stones of the less frequented streets, and along the straight road called the King's Dam, which led for two miles over the marshes, and up the long hill bordered by an occasional cluster or row of cottages, to the bit of lonely road between hedges which led to the gates of Waringham Park. Geraldine was rather pleased by the unexpected warmth with which the selfish Miss Eleanor, who had missed her small attentions and her youthful presence, welcomed her back; but the invalid had no eyes for the changes in other people than herself, and Geraldine's increased gravity was as much lost upon her as upon her more frigid sister. Dinner was over early, and, the evening being warm and fine, and the girl mad to escape from the vault and its ghosts—her own irreverent private names for the house and its mistresses—she went into the garden, and, being tired, restless, and unhappy, she could not confine herself to her favourite "rose-corner" or the hedged-in monotony of the grass-walk, but traversed the latter quickly and dived into the wood at the farther end. She went on and on along the narrow path, brushing her way through the tall grass that grew in summer luxuriance on both sides, and pushing aside the branches that straggled forward from the young trees on either hand, until she reached the outer hedge and the gate at the end of the path which opened on to the high-road.

There she stopped, and, with her hand upon the wooden bars, looked out over the quiet road at the stretch of sloping fields beyond and at the low hills in the distance which bounded the prospect. The sweet peace of the summer evening gave her no pleasure, for she was not in the mood to be pleased; her eyes moved restlessly over the pretty scene, her fingers tapped the gate in impatience. She had been standing there for some minutes when a man's voice made her start.

"Lovely view, isn't it, Miss Lindley?"

Captain Morrison was standing in the road a few feet from the gate ; she blushed, uneasily wondering how long he had been watching her.

" Lovely ? I don't think so. I'm tired of the stagnant country. I begin to hate the sight of a field or a tree."

" You used not to speak so ; your visit to town has spoilt you." He raised his eyes slowly, with a certain appearance of reserved shyness usual to him, to her face ; but they rested there for a moment with a look of shrewd penetration which impressed her with a sudden fear that he could read more of her thoughts than she wished to have known. " It has made you discontented and unhappy," he went on boldly.

" You think the gaiety and dissipation of town have done that ?" she asked, failing, however, to speak as lightly as she wished to do.

He paused for a moment, during which she waited for his next words with some uneasiness.

" No," he replied at last, in his monotonous and measured voice, " I think that sorrow and disappointment have done so."

"What do you mean?" she broke out quickly.

" That I have guessed, that I am sure an errand of mercy and kindness took you to town, and that you made there the bitter discovery that those feelings were unmerited by the object of them."

She attempted to speak, in great agitation ; she wished to laugh at his suggestion and to show resentment at his boldness; but she broke down at the first word, and fell into passionate silence, her bosom heaving, her eyes filling with tears. He came forward and laid his hand on hers, not with loverlike impetuosity, but firmly and respectfully, as she was about to turn away from the gate.

" I entreat you not to be offended with me for my boldness. Remember, this is a subject on which you have shown me some confidence before. You are not one of those frivolous girls who allow themselves to be much elated or depressed about trifles. You have confessed to the deepest solicitude concerning your adopted brother——"

"Brother?" she interrupted proudly. "I

have no brother, and there is no man in the world whom I look upon as a brother. Please don't let us talk about it; don't say I have mentioned the subject to you. I will never, if I can help it, mention his name again."

" Then you have satisfied yourself of his guilt ? You know where he is hiding ? You have seen him perhaps ? "

Now, although she stood with lips firmly closed and made no verbal answer to these questions, her very attitude was a sufficient reply to them.

" You may think my interest strange, perhaps impertinent," said he; " but I have myself suffered in much the same way through the misconduct of—a member of my own family, and I can sympathize with every feeling you have in the matter. But I go farther than you do. You wish to bury your—disappointment; I keep mine alive."

There was a quiet determination about the little man, as he let these words drop in the lowest, most monotonous of voices, that made him seem to her quite terrible.

" But that is not right," said she.

He did not answer ; but she instinctively
knew that no protest, however powerful, would
have the least effect upon his stubborn earnestness.

" At least," he remarked presently, his tone
suddenly becoming very gentle, " you believe
that I deeply sympathize with you."

" I have no need of sympathy, thank you,"
she retorted, rather ungraciously, offended at
the suggestion that the conduct of such a man
as James had proved to be could have any effect
upon her.   " I was sorry for my guardian's
nephew when I thought he was accused wrong-
fully ; but I have no pity for the guilty," she
added, with the inexorable sternness of inex-
perience.

But he, the man of thirty-five, looked at her
sceptically ; to him the depth of expression in
her eyes when she was excited, the firm lines
already to be seen about the mouth, were more
eloquent than her impulsive words.

" A silly fellow, to forfeit the right to this
pretty place—and—and all the charms it
contains ! " he observed, looking up at the trees.

" I don't see any charm in it ; I hate the

place ; the house is a tomb ; the very air one seems to breathe with difficulty ; and the garden is—haunted," said she, shuddering.

" Then why do you stay in it ? You might certainly find plenty of opportunities to get away," he responded slowly and significantly.

" How ? " asked she, not understanding him in the least.

" There are plenty of people who would be only too delighted to rescue you from your prison, and to surround you with every pleasure the world can afford."

His tone was so measured, and this insinuation came upon her so unexpectedly, that his full meaning did not dawn upon her even now. It was not until he came a step nearer and deliberately took her hands in his and held them so firmly that it was of no use to attempt to escape, that, with horror which appeared comically in her face, she found that she was listening to a proposal of marriage.

" Only say where you would like to go, what life you would like to lead, and, if you will trust your happiness to me, I will deny you no wish ; I will devote my whole life to making yours sweet to you. Won't you listen to me? You will never find a man to love you more than I do."

She did listen, with the liveliest and the strangest sensation with which a woman ever heard a love-suit. When she had recovered from the first shock of astonishment and absolute fright, it occurred to her, not as in the case of Reginald Bamber, that her suitor was incapable of deep devotion, but that he was using its formulas to express feelings which no longer animated him, or which, at any rate, were not inspired by her. Her first impulse was to reject him at once unconditionally; and her tone betrayed her intention with her first words—

"I am very much flattered—I am very grateful; but I have no thought of—— "

He interrupted her with a burst of genuine earnestness which astonished her more than ever—

"I implore you not to refuse me at once. I know I have surprised you, you want time for consideration ; take what time you please—till to-morrow—till next week ; but don't refuse me now ; let me at least hope a little longer."

He was eager enough now; he absolutely would not let the discouraging words she had ready pass her lips, but turned the talk at once into another channel by asking after the two old ladies. She answered his questions rather timidly, being unable to recover so quickly as he from the emotion caused by that strange interlude ; but when at last she prepared to go back to the house and held out her hand to him, he retained it while he whispered, his dark eyes lighting up with eagerness—

" You will not forget, you will not forget? And you will not be too cruel! When shall I come to receive your answer? To-morrow? May I come here to-morrow evening? If you are here at this time to-morrow, I shall know I may hope."

Before she could protest, with one more pressure of the hand, one more eloquent look out of his great eyes, which had the wistful look of a dumb animal in moments of pleading, he retreated so quickly that, when he raised his hat, he was already too far off for her to give him a discouraging answer.

CHAPTER VIII.

GERALDINE turned and ran back to the house, too much excited for steady walking. As she was flying, in the same rather wild manner, through the hall, Miss Elizabeth met her and asked what was the matter.

"Oh, nothing," she replied—"at least, Captain Morrison has—I met him at the gate of the wood. I've been talking to him."

"He has proposed to you?"

"Why, how did you guess?"

"Not a very difficult task when a gentleman shows such devotion as Captain Morrison has done."

"But I don't think he has; his offer took me quite by surprise. I know he has been here a good deal; but his talk, his manner, never suggested even admiration."

"Well, I suppose you are satisfied on that point now ? "

"I don't know ; I don't think I care."

" My dear child, I hope you have not been so foolish as to refuse him ? "

" I—I think so. It—it never occurred to me to accept him. He wants me to consider it ; but——"

She stopped of her own accord. Not until this moment had it occurred to her that the matter required consideration. Her hesitation was enough for the penetrating eyes fixed upon her.

"Unless you dislike him, my dear, it is worth considering," said she, not too earnestly. " For we know from half a dozen people that he is unusually well off for a soldier, and has expectations besides. The admiral can't say enough about his character too. It is a matter entirely for your own judgment, of course, dear ; but it is certainly a flattering offer."

She let the girl go, afraid of saying too much on a subject more vitally interesting to her than it seemed at present to Geraldine herself. Now that the much-abused vagrant

was her formally adopted niece, Elizabeth recognized the advantages of the connection, and,
identifying the girl's interests with those of the
family, was eager for her satisfactory establish-
ment.

So Geraldine went up to her own room and
" considered it."   If Captain Morrison had
made his offer a week before, it would have
been at once rejected ; but it had come just at
the right time, when disgust with a man who
had certainly occupied a large share of her
thoughts had been succeeded by a blank feeling
of sudden aimlessness in her life, and by an
irritable longing to break up the old conditions
of it.   And here was the opportunity of doing
so, of leaving the gloomy house which recalled
at every step memories of the two deepest
sorrows of her life, her guardian's death and
James's wickedness—of escaping from the
uncongenial, maddeningly monotonous society
of her adopted aunts—of seeing some of the
beautiful places she longed to see.   And all
this with only one drawback, an insignificant
one that quite threatened to be overlooked at
first, as she reckoned up the advantages of the

prospect; this was the man she would have to love, honour, and obey for the rest of her life. Her life—yes, there was something appalling about that; but then other girls were continually promising the same thing, and they seemed to get on all right. Geraldine was obliged to look at the subject in this way, from the outside, because her heart was not touched. She wondered whether, this being the case, she ought to allow the matter to enter into her consideration at all; but then, after having refused kind, handsome Reginald Bamber so easily, she had come to the decision that she was very cold by nature, and could never expect to feel the raptures that some girls did in these cases.

And even the man himself was not in any way obnoxious to her; she was rather afraid of him, indeed; but it was with a fear very different from that inspired by Reginald—the fear a girl unused to much society naturally has for a reserved man whom she does not know very well; a fear, therefore, which would probably wear off with marriage. He seemed more human, too, than Reginald, less invariably

correct in judgment, more prone to passion
and prejudice under all his reserve, and the
report had also reached her that he was a
"devil in action."

Therefore, on the evening after his proposal,
after much nervous hesitation, and even one or
two undecided turns to and from the house,
she at last sauntered into the wood-path with
lagging, lingering feet, and would perhaps
never have reached the gate at the end of
it, if Captain Morrison had not anticipated
her reluctant arrival and trespassed into the
wood to meet her. And that meeting decided
the question. He had prepared some appro-
priate eloquence wherewith to turn the balance
of her indecision; and she returned to the
house under promise to be his wife.

Elizabeth was delighted. Poor Reginald,
who called next day to tell the news that he
had given up all thought of returning to
America just yet, and had accepted a post in
London less lucrative than that he was to have
held in New York, in order to be less far from
—from Waringham, was visibly affected out of
his usual placidity by the announcement made

by Elizabeth of Geraldine's engagement. The girl guiltily avoided a *tête-à-tête* with him, feeling that she had not treated him quite well ; but it could not be put off for ever, and her evasion of it made his words the more impressive on the afternoon when he at last caught her in the park alone.

She kept the talk to common-places as long as she could, but some reference to her engagement was of course inevitable.

"I hear you are to be married very soon ? "

"Yes. Captain Morrison has to go to Vienna, and he wants me to marry him first."

"Of course. You will find it very hot there still, won't you ? "

"I don't know ; it will be early in September." A pause. "I have always longed to travel."

Another pause ; perhaps he was thinking rather bitterly of her refusal to travel with him. They were both becoming fearfully nervous.

"You made up your mind very suddenly, didn't you ? " he asked, with a lugubrious attempt to speak playfully. "We poor civilians can't hope to compete with military impetuosity; where we humbly and vaguely beg on our knees, the soldier simply says 'Surrender!' and the thing is done."

"Captain Morrison didn't; and no civilian ever begged anything of me on his knees."

"Geraldine," said he—he had always called her "Miss Lindley," but now that she was lost to him he was less punctiliously civil, more friendly and affectionate—"you know how earnestly I wished for your happiness. I think you give me credit for not being wholly selfish in my motives; you may indeed. Captain Morrison is not a friend of mine— you are; therefore there is no disloyalty, and, believe me, there is as little mean jealousy as I can help, in what I am going to say. Do not let them hurry you into this marriage; insist upon taking your own time, and learn all you can about your future husband and his connections; don't be too proud even to make inquiries, to ask questions and sift the answers."

"How can I do that? How can I show such a want of confidence?" she asked restlessly, impressed in spite of herself by his earnest manner. " I have accepted him, I have almost fixed the day; I cannot ferret out his history, I cannot draw back now."

He seemed appalled by the swiftness with which step after step in such an important matter had been taken, and for a moment his alarm infected her. She laughed foolishly as she curled up a leaf of the rose she was carrying with trembling fingers; she was on the point of trying to turn the subject to one less portentous, when he stopped her by saying, with all the earnestness in his power—

" I cannot say more to you. I frankly own that I have nothing but suspicion to go upon; but it is a suspicion which makes me shudder. You refused me on the plea that I was 'too good'; pray Heaven you may not have a different fault to find with the husband you have chosen ! "

His voice was shaking; without another word, he raised his hat and hurried away, leaving her in a state of agitation which she had scarcely controlled by the time her lover arrived. He had met Reginald at the park-gates, and had not been at all pleased to see him; and now, seeing that something was wrong with Geraldine, that her manner was cool and even mistrustful, he put down this change, with great acumen, to the man whom he knew to have been his unsuccessful rival.

"What has Mr. Bamber been telling you about me, Geraldine?" he asked, putting his hand on her shoulder gently enough, but looking neither very loving nor very good-tempered.

"Nothing," she answered, of course, with a start. She persisted in this statement; so Captain Morrison, seeing that he was only rousing, to no purpose, a dangerous spirit of resistance, said at last, as if satisfied—

"That's all right, then. I shouldn't have teased you about this, my darling, if I had not been told that Mr. Bamber had vowed that, if you would not have him, at least, if he could help it, you shouldn't be happy with me."

"Oh, Philip, I don't believe he would say such a thing!" she exclaimed.

But an affianced husband has advantages and privileges wherewith, if he use them with discernment, he may destroy a rival's credit in a girl's not wholly unprejudiced mind to the increase of his own ; and, before he bade farewell to Geraldine that evening, Philip Morrison had not only persuaded her to hasten the day of happiness by a whole week, but had almost induced her to believe that Reginald Bamber, in his advice and his warnings, had not been wholly uninfluenced by an unworthy readiness to avail himself of some trifling fault or other which it had come to his knowledge that his rival or one of his relatives had committed at some period or other of their lives. This was the only conclusion she could come to, for she was too loyal to repeat to her lover the words or the substance of her friend's warning.

And so, after an engagement of five weeks, Captain Morrison and Geraldine Lindley were married, in as private a manner as possible, in consequence of Sir Charles's death, at the little church between the park-gates and the Vicarage. The ceremony was performed by old Mr. Cox of Copsley ; no one was present except old Mr. Bamber and Mrs. Bamber, Mr. Meadows, who assisted in the service, the parish clerk, Mr. and Mrs. Corbyn, and the

whole of the Waringham household. Miss
Gretton was not well enough to come; but she
sent a lugubrious present of Young's "Night
Thoughts," beautifully bound, and a pair of jet
bracelets.

Then at the Hall there was a rather solemn
luncheon, with Mr. and Mrs. Bamber as the
only guests. Geraldine was very silent, and
seemed to be only just awakening to a sense
of the seriousness of the step she had taken;
but she was far too highly strung up to cry.
The only two persons who wept much were
Miss Eleanor and Mrs. Symes, the latter of
whom, oppressed by the sight of a wedding
shorn of its proper festivities, made the unhappy
remark that " it upset her more than poor dear
Sir Charles's funeral—that it did!" But she
recovered sufficiently to throw a pound or so
of rice, in a weak and wavering way, in at the
window of the barouche as it started on its way
to Goldborough station; and she considered
it a lucky omen that some of it went into the
bridegroom's eyes; but he did not see it in the
same light, and gave way under his breath to
a bad military habit as he looked sharply out

of the window and met her inane smile of satisfaction ; and this omen was not so good.

Geraldine was not superstitious ; moreover, she was glad to leave the gloomy old house which had been her home for the last four months ; but, when her husband suddenly started up in the carriage, declaring that he had lost a locket which was more precious to him than life, and eager to turn back to hunt for it, and when she picked up from the floor of the carriage a little shield-shaped medallion, which had opened in the fall, showing the portrait of a young and beautiful woman, Reginald Bamber's despised warning flashed across her mind, and she wondered, with a shiver of dread, whether there might not be worse trials in store for her than the endurance of sad memories in the peaceful, if monotonous, shelter of Waringham Hall.

CHAPTER IX.

THE newly-married pair were to be away two
or three months, travelling about, spending
some time in Vienna, Paris, and probably a few
weeks at Nice or Mentone towards the end
of the year. They had not yet decided on
their future place of residence; but Captain
Morrison had made the proposal that, as he
should certainly have to return to England from
time to time for a day or two on business, he
should appoint an agent to look out for him,
should inspect, during his short visits, the houses
likely to suit him, and, having chosen one,
should give orders for it to be furnished and
got ready for his final home-coming with his
wife at the end of the year.

But they had scarcely been a month away,
when, in the first days of October, having

received one or two short and uninteresting
letters from the bride in the course of the
honeymoon, Miss Elizabeth was startled by
the receipt of a telegram sent by Captain
Morrison, stating that he and his wife were on
the way to England, and that they were coming
straight to Waringham Hall. Preparations
were hastily made; the room which had been
Sir Charles's was got ready for them, the ladies
and the housekeeper put on gowns of state,
the barouche was sent to meet every train as
soon as it was possible for them to arrive.
They came by the express which, leaving
Liverpool Street at five in the afternoon,
reached Goldborough at twenty-three minutes
past eight.

It was dark when Jo, the gardener's boy,
stationed at the lodge to give notice of the
arrival of the travellers, ran panting up to the
garden to give the news to the servants waiting
about there, who passed it on to those indoors,
till Johnson announced to the ladies in the
drawing-room that Captain and Mrs. Morrison
were driving through the park. There was
intense excitement in all the household. Every

rheumatic old servant seemed galvanized into
activity; the gardener, the under-gardener, and
Jo made as imposing a display as they could
of themselves at the entrance of the garden;
the servants were drawn up in a line in the
outer hall, which was decked with evergreens
and the best of the camellias, brought in from
the conservatory and disposed with as much
effect as possible round the hall stove.   When
the barouche stopped at the entrance, Johnson
was already smiling in his blandest manner at
the wide-open door, Miss Eleanor and Miss
Elizabeth were in sight, ready with an effusive
welcome.

Geraldine came in quickly, with flushed face
and glittering eyes, and with subdued excitement in her manner which strengthened
Elizabeth's acute suspicion that something was
wrong.   No one else noticed this.   Every
member of the household, from Eleanor to the
lowest kitchenmaid, was impressed by an altera-
tion in "Miss Geraldine" which in their eyes
was all improvement; it was typified by the
change from the simple travelling-dress in which
she had started on her bridal tour to one no

less simple indeed, but with the artistic simplicity
of Worth replacing the more modest simplicity
of the Goldborough dressmaker. Her husband
was honoured with very little of the general
attention. Again no one but Elizabeth noticed
that, while even more taciturn than usual at
dinner, which was served immediately, his
manner was restless and absent, and he was
so nervous that he started like a delicate woman
at any unexpected sound. Geraldine made up
for her husband's silence by an unfailing stream
of bright chatter about the places and people
she had seen, which delighted and amused the
old ladies, who seldom heard so much of the
outer world.

After dinner she sang them an Italian
peasant's song she had learned, and played
them some new waltzes. Then it was that she
proposed to them an arrangement which was
all they desired, and which Miss Elizabeth had
hinted at before the wedding. It was that
Captain Morrison should rent the Hall from the
trustees, make what improvements he pleased,
and so restore its ancient prestige.

"My dear Geraldine, I think nothing could

be better!" agreed Elizabeth, with sparkling
eyes. "I long to see a little life and youth
about the place again."

"Oh, we shan't be very gay!" said Geraldine, laughing nervously, and glancing rather
furtively at her husband. "We have had
enough gaiety for the present, and shall be
quiet enough. Things will go on around you
much as usual."

"Then you will not mind our remaining?
We could take a small place near, you know, if
we were likely to be in your way."

"But you are not, you are not; we want
you to stay; don't you understand?" cried
Geraldine, impatiently.

After the excitement of travel and the
exertion she had made since her arrival to
be bright and lively, she was getting quite
feverish. At last, when the clock had struck
eleven, an hour long past the usual time for
the old ladies to retire, and they were both
growing so sleepy that it was impossible for
her to detain them any longer, she crossed the
room with Miss Elizabeth, and, holding her
back as the elder passed out, she said, in a low

voice, with a nervous glance at her husband,
who had returned to his armchair after lighting
their candles for them—

"What made you put us in that room? It
makes me nervous; I shall not be able to sleep
there."

"Well, my dear, it is the largest and most
comfortable room upstairs. But, of course, if
you and Captain Morrison—Philip—don't like
it——"

"He won't mind, I dare say," she interrupted, with a shrug of her shoulders.
"Couldn't you let me sleep with you, just for
to-night?"

"My dear, the servants would think it so
strange!" urged Elizabeth, shocked.

"Oh, very well!" she said uncertainly, still
with her hand upon the handle of the door, in
front of the elder lady. The partition between
the larger and the smaller drawing-rooms, which
had once been divided by folding-doors, kept
her out of sight of her husband. Elizabeth's
penetrating look seemed to demand an explanation. "Philip has had bad news of some kind
or other, I think; at least he decided very

suddenly to come back to England, and said it
was 'business;' and since then he has been so
dreadfully nervous and restless, he infects me
with it; and we are both always jumping and
starting like a pair of marionettes," said she,
laughing almost hysterically.

"But, my dear Geraldine, he is your
husband; surely your presence soothes him,
and it is the duty of a wife——"

"To keep out of her husband's way when
her presence only irritates him and his irritates
her.   However, I dare say we shall work
better in double harness before long!" she
added, with an effort at brightness which
sounded painfully flippant to the scandalized
maiden lady.

"My dear, I really think you are too hard
upon a husband who seems to try to please you
in every way," said she, in a whisper, feeling
bound to deliver some sort of lecture, now that
the young wife's undutiful talk had frightened
away her sleepiness. "He is certainly rather
taciturn; but he seems to have taken you
everywhere and given you everything you
wanted."

"Yes, because he likes excitement, and is too proud not to have his wife well-dressed."

"Well, well, so much the better for you! Then he takes the deepest interest in your family; only this evening he asked in the most solicitous manner if we had had any tidings of poor James."

She stopped, appalled. Geraldine's face had suddenly become convulsed with terror as she seized the elder lady's hands, trying to speak, but failing at first through the dryness of her mouth. Between them they dropped the candle, and, as the younger picked it up, Captain Morrison appeared from behind the partition.

"What are you hissing and whispering about, Geraldine?" he asked irritably. "You can come into the room if you have anything to say, can't you, instead of keeping Miss Elizabeth in the draught?"

It was the first complaining speech he had made to his wife that evening; but then, too, it was almost the first time he had addressed her. She answered with meekness which always marked her bearing towards him, but which did not seem to please him—

"I have nothing more to say, Philip; I was only talking about the room upstairs."

He shot at her a furtive glance of suspicion, and remained with her at the door while Elizabeth, with another good-night kiss, followed her sister upstairs.

Now Miss Elizabeth Otway was by no means a nervous woman, nor one prone to make a mountain of dread of a mole-hill of doubt; nevertheless, the results of her observation of the newly-married pair that evening, and of that short colloquy with the young wife, were not only to cause her to look forward with some anxiety to the future, but also to send her to her room with an uncomfortable feeling that some sort of immediate danger hung over the present. There was a sharp turn in the corridor between her room and that which had been prepared for the young couple. She heard in a few minutes the soft shutting of the door, and guessed that Geraldine had come upstairs; and soon after she heard footsteps and the dressing-room door shut, and it was plain that Captain Morrison had come up too; and presently she fancied she heard the sounds of voices,

and, though her ears were very keen, it was
plain that either her imagination led her away,
or they must be talking very excitedly to be
heard at all at this distance. She sat down as
usual to read her " Bogatsky " and the evening-
lessons ; and, while still so engaged, she raised
her head sharply, convinced at last that the one
high note which pierced the night-silence was
either a woman's scream or some passionately-
spoken word in an outbreak of a woman's fierce
excitement. She crossed her room quickly,
book in hand, unlocked her door, and listened.
In a few moments she heard murmurs, now
soft, now loud, undistinguishable always ; then
the man's voice rising higher, some sound
louder still, which made Elizabeth start forward
with clenched hand ; then the door-handle
rattled, and, as the door was flung open, she
clearly heard Captain Morrison's voice saying,
not loudly, but in sharp, distinct tones—

" For Heaven's sake, stay here; I won't
hurt you ; I won't frighten you. Don't go
and alarm the house."

" Let me go, or I'll cry out ! " hissed Geraldine.

And the next moment a flying figure appeared at the turn of the corridor, and Elizabeth, coming out of her room and whispering, "What is it—what is it?" received the panting woman in her arms.

"Sh—don't cry out; come in here!" she said, drew Geraldine into her own room, and locked the door.

She would not let her speak at once, but, placing her in the armchair from which she herself had just risen, she bathed her damp and ghastly face with eau-de-Cologne. For Geraldine seemed on the point of fainting; her white skin had no trace of colour; her quivering lips were parted, and her dark eyes were fixed vacantly in front of her, as she leant back in the chair, with waxen hands hanging limply down, and submitted inertly to the elder lady's ministrations.

"Did he strike you?" asked Elizabeth, in a whisper, when at last Geraldine said mechanically, "Thank you," and raised her head from the back of the chair.

"Oh, no—worse, worse—much worse!"

"My dear Geraldine, what did he do? Tell

me quickly, for Heaven's sake!" And her fancy flew to Desdemona and tales of midnight murder.

She shook her head and sat up, while Elizabeth was reassured but still more puzzled by noticing that her pale pink cashmere dressing-gown, with its frills and folds of lace, showed no traces of rough handling, and her chestnut hair, hanging down in two plaits, little sign of disorder. Geraldine began to laugh hysterically as she suffered this inspection.

"Oh, I'm not hurt—at least, I have no bruises or broken bones!" Then, as Elizabeth drew herself up stiffly, as if feeling that she had been tricked, she added—"I have only found out what I have suspected for the last ten days—what the man is that I have married."

"What he is!"

"Yes; I have found out why the little show of affection he made me before marriage has disappeared so quickly, why he evidently had but one object in my society, why our honeymoon was spent in erratic rushes from one place to another, and backwards and

forwards between them." She looked up at
Miss Elizabeth, and paused. These two had
never really been friends. The younger could
never forget the cruelty with which she had
been received on her first visit to Waringham
Hall; the elder still treasured up the memory
of the wrong which Sir Charles's caprice had
done to herself and her sister. A moment of
terror had made the one kind, the other
confiding; but already sympathy had given
place in the face of the elder lady to hard,
eager curiosity; already a spirit of caution led
the younger to measure her words. " He is
mad ! " she ended briefly.

At that moment there was a knock at the
door, and Captain Morrison's voice called
softly—

" Geraldine ! "

She started, but did not answer.

" I will speak to him ; I'm not afraid," said
Elizabeth ; and, arming herself with the biggest
book of devotion which lay on the chest of
drawers, she unlocked and cautiously opened
the door. He looked as sane as a man can,
more composed than he had been all the

evening; the most imaginative person could have discovered no sign of frenzy in face, voice, or manner. If he had been mad, the paroxysm was over. He looked naturally somewhat annoyed at the errand which brought him; but even his annoyance was well under control.

"I am very sorry to disturb you at this time of night, Miss Elizabeth, but I think I heard my wife's voice."

"Yes, she is in here."

"Will you ask her to come and speak to me? Tell her I don't want to hurt her, as she seems—the Lord knows why—to imagine, and that I hope to goodness she doesn't want to make another scene. If the servants should get wind of this midnight amusement of coursing through the passage and playing hide-and-seek in other people's rooms, we shall never hear the end of it."

This he said in a low, distinct voice, all for the benefit of his wife, whom he could not see. Elizabeth, who was no coward, ashamed of her weapon, let her book of devotions slide down upon the floor.

"She seems to be afraid of you," she

observed dryly, annoyed with the young wife
for this escapade.

"Yes, I haven't the least notion why; I
believe Sir Charles's room made her nervous.
She had better sleep with you to-night, I think,
if you will let her; but I must speak to her
first.   Here, you may tie my hands together,
if she is afraid of me," he added, with a look
up at Miss Elizabeth and a backward nod of
the head as much as to say, " Did you ever
hear such nonsense?"—which had the desired
effect of enlisting the valiant elderly lady on
his side, in disgust at the young wife's fanciful
terrors.

"Geraldine," she called in a cold voice,
turning to the chair in which the frightened
woman sat, listening intently with wide eyes
and parted lips, " Philip is here.   He wishes
to speak to you."

She rose obediently and came slowly to the
door.

"Come out here.   I must speak to you;
I won't touch you."

For one moment she hesitated, her bosom
heaving, her face eloquent—not with fear, but

disgust; then, glancing at Elizabeth's hard,
unsympathetic face, she saw there was no help
for it, and went out into the corridor.

"What have you told her?"

"Nothing—at least not all."

"What are you going to tell her?"

"Nothing more."

"There's a sensible woman!" in a tone of
great relief.

"But it shall be told. Every one shall
know. I will get freed from you," she hissed
out in the whisper she was bound to maintain,
but boldly and fiercely.

"That's right! Nothing could serve me
better! It is the first time you have shown me
any spirit," said he coolly.

She was too angry to answer. If her spirit
had slumbered till this moment, it was awake
now; and the steady look of hatred she gave
him in the feeble light of the candle over which
he was blinking would have assured a less
careless observer that in her dealings with him
she would never lack it again. So she returned
abruptly to Elizabeth's room, and, wishing that
lady good night, made her way to one of the

spare rooms which was always ready for use;
while Captain Morrison, after exchanging a
few remarks and shrugs with Elizabeth upon
young ladies' caprices, sauntered slowly back
to his room.

Next morning, at breakfast, nothing seemed
wrong, except that Geraldine, who was again
very talkative and lively, was ghastly pale.
She passed the morning quietly in unpacking
her trunks, and in showing her husband's
presents and her own purchases, which were
numerous and costly enough to have reconciled
most young ladies to the galling chain of
matrimony, to her adopted aunts. Captain
Morrison remained until luncheon-time in the
library, writing letters. At that meal,
Geraldine's spirits rose to such an hysterical
height that her husband suggested that she
would be tired out long before the day was
over if she did not lie down and rest as soon
as they left the table; and, with the meekness
with which she invariably took every hint of
his, she went upstairs as soon as they left the
dining-room.

But half an hour later Miss Eleanor, who

was slowly going upstairs, met Geraldine coming
down in walking-dress.

"Where are you going, dear? I wanted
you to come and read to me; but I did not
like to ask, as I thought you were going to lie
down."

"I am going into the grass-walk, Aunt
Eleanor. I think that will do my head more
good than lying down."

"Oh, I didn't know you had a headache,
dear! Come to my room, and I will give you
some of the mixture Mr. Crosse gave me, that
always does my head so much good."

"Thank you. I—I mustn't come now.
I—the fact is, I don't want Philip to see I am
disobeying him."

And, stooping to kiss the little withered
face very tenderly, and dropping a tear as she
did so on the shawl of her astonished aunt, she
ran downstairs past her, through the halls,
opened and shut the front door very softly,
and, sauntering through the rose-corner with
feet which would go fast in spite of her, she
got into the grass-walk; and there, secure from
view between the tall hedges, she ran as if for

life, and then tore her way through the wood-
path to that gate of evil memory where Philip
Morrison had proposed to her.   She shuddered
with disgust at her own weakness as she passed
through it, and found herself fairly started on
her dangerous walk.   For there was only one
road by which she could reach Goldborough ;
and her husband, about whose arrangements
for the afternoon she had not dared to ask,
might take it into his head to ride or drive
into the town ; and, if he should overtake her
when she was crossing the marsh, there was no
hope of her being able to hide from him.   It
was about three miles from Waringham Hall
to Goldborough station, which lay at the bottom
of a hill on the other side of the town.   The
London train she wanted to catch left Goldborough at 4.31, arriving at Liverpool Street
exactly at eight.   It was now very little past
three, and she had therefore plenty of time ;
but she was far too nervous to be able to realize
that and to plod steadily on in an unsuspicious
manner.   The faintest sound of hoofs or wheels
in the distance behind her made her turn and
look anxiously back ; every five minutes she

would pull out her watch, and reckon how much time she had to spare. She had, besides her husband, her acquaintances to fear. If she were to meet any one who was at all intimate either with her or the Otways, she would certainly be detained, and made to give an explanation of this lonely walk on the very day after her return from her wedding-tour; worse than that, she might meet some one who had not heard of her return.

She was fortunate, however. She saw a carriage she knew in advance of her, and loitered until it was a long way off; and, at a point where her road was crossed by another, she saw a gentleman on horseback riding away from her, whom she believed to be Reginald Bamber; but she did not see him turn round. The long, open, willow-bordered road over the marsh she crossed in safety, but in deadly fear, uttered a thanksgiving as she reached the outskirts of the town, crossed the bridge by the timber-yard, toiled up the long hill to the market-place, and almost ran down the gradual decline which led to the station. Thank Heaven, she was in time! She had to wait

a quarter of an hour before the ticket-office would
be open, and this time she spent, in suspense
which seemed to hold her breath, in the wretched
country waiting-room. When at last she had
taken her ticket and hurried out on to the platform to watch for the train, she felt that the
worst was already over, and her heart gave a
bound of triumph. At the very moment of this
premature elation, a voice behind her saying,
"Welcome to Norfolk, Mrs. Morrison!" caused
her to give a start which proclaimed her guilt,
even before she turned and, with a face from
which the flush of excitement had suddenly
died out, shook hands with Reginald Bamber.

He was perfectly sweet, perfectly calm as
usual—seemed to see nothing extraordinary
in the most awkward and spasmodic greeting
that any woman but a raw school-girl ever
offered a man. He held in his hand a couple
of London papers as the ostensible reason of
his coming to the station; but neither his
manner nor his ostentatious *Standard* and
World deceived her. She knew that he had
seen, watched, and followed her, and her spirit
rose in arms against him for his impertinence.

"I heard that you were expected yesterday; but I did not hope to have the pleasure of meeting you so soon—and here too!"

"I came to get a paper; I hope you haven't bought them all up, Mr. Bamber," said she, recovering herself.

"No, not quite. Which shall I get for you?" he asked, picking up her ticket, which she had dropped, and handing it to her, still without the least surprise.

But her coolness could not stand such a test; she took the ticket with trembling fingers and thanked him, without meeting his eyes.

"I am afraid you have done too much travelling about," he remarked, just in the same tone, but in a rather lower voice. "You don't look so well as when you left Waringham, Mrs. Morrison."

"Yes, we went to too many places and saw too many things," she answered quickly; "and, when we were in Paris, we were at the theatre every night."

"Ah, and all that tells! But of course, in Paris and on a honeymoon, it is difficult to be moderate in enjoyment."

Her face broke up as she gave him a glance which moved him out of his tranquillity,

"Enjoyment!" she sobbed, with the long-withheld tears rolling down her cheeks.

"Come into the station," said he, in exactly the same soft voice as usual; and he led the way into the empty waiting-room in such an unmoved, sauntering fashion that it attracted no remark, and Geraldine's tears, falling fast beneath her veil, also escaped notice, as he continued to talk commonplaces about over-fatigue and modern facilities for travel, till they stood alone in the dusty room.

"Don't cry," he said kindly, taking out his pocket-knife and cutting the *World*. "If any Waringham people were to come in they would think it so odd."

"I don't care what Waringham people think!" flashed out Geraldine, the very suggestion that she could care for such a trifle causing the tears to cease. "I don't care if every cottager in Waringham were to be on the platform to see me cry my eyes out as I go off, for I shall never see them again."

"But there are other people to be considered

besides the cottagers. You haven't married the cottagers, you know," continued Reginald, still cutting his paper.

"What are you trying to find out, Mr. Bamber?" she asked coldly.

"Why you are running away, of course, Mrs. Morrison."

She stopped his pen-knife impatiently and made him meet her eyes; but his own were as calm and as kind as usual.

"Why do you pretend you don't know, when all the time you do know? And why do you try to stop me now—for you are trying to stop me, though you shall not succeed—when it was your duty to have saved me before, not by giving me a vague warning which no girl could take, but by telling me the whole truth?"

"I did tell you all I knew—all I know now."

She paused and looked penetratingly at him.

"And that is——"

"That he is a fanatic, a man with one idea, and therefore not likely to make any woman happy."

"You did not know what that idea was— you could not, or you would have told me.

You cannot have known either why he married
me."

"I didn't think that wanted an explanation,"
said he simply.

"If you had known his reason, you would
not have believed it; it was too monstrous—
too horrible! He is not a man; he is a demon!"

Reginald lookèd at her in rising alarm; he
was not so much afraid of some terrible dis-
closure as afraid that she was losing her wits.

"What would you say to a man who had
devoted his life to hounding another man down,
who had deliberately chosen for himself as a
pursuit, as a pastime, the office of blood-hound,
to display his ingenuity and his keenness where
professional detectives had failed; who began
his self-appointed task by sneaking down to
the neighbourhood of the home of the man he
was hunting, worming himself into the confidence of the man's friends, trying to ferret out
from them the poor wretch's hiding-place?
What would you say, if, failing in this, this spy,
having found out that the information he wanted
was in the hands of a girl who could not be
cajoled into giving it up, had made up his

mind to marry her, in the certainty that, with the authority which only marriage gives, he could sooner or later wrench the secret from her ? "

Reginald was startled at last, but it was into utter incredulity.

" Listen, listen ! What I am telling you is true. What would you say, if the newly-married bride, from her husband's coldness and from the persistency with which he kept to one subject, had her suspicions roused, and found that on this, her very wedding-tour, her husband was following the track of this man, a man whom she had loved as if he had been her own brother ? What would you say to that ? What would you say ? "

" Why, that it was impossible—-that there was some strange mistake somewhere ! "

" But it is not impossible—it is true," she averred, falling from eager volubility into impressive, slow earnestness. " When I heard here and there, on our tour, the name of Sir James Otway, when I found that the man I had married could find interest with me in no other subject, I began to think, I began to

watch; and, when I found that, as soon as
Captain Morrison learnt that Sir James had
returned to England, he found that 'business'
called him back, I felt sure; and last night—
think what a home-coming for a newly-married
wife!—he was tired and angry at my changed
manner, and, I suppose, off his guard, for, when
I accused him quite unexpectedly, the very
manner in which he met my words betrayed
him, and he swore to my face that the law
should never claim James Otway, that he would
never rest till he had tracked him down and—
and killed him like a dog!"

Her voice was going, her last words were
hoarsely and feebly spoken; but the fire in her
eyes was not that of insanity; and, when she
had finished, she waited, with dead calmness
after her passionate outburst, for his answer.

The London train had come and gone, two
or three passengers had rushed into the room
and out again while she poured forth her story;
she had not heeded, but he had; and he had
stood before her that she might not be seen
and recognized as she looked steadily up at him
with her passion-lit eyes, her face distorted with

burning excitement. When she at last paused,
he was as calm as ever; but he looked very,
very grave.

" Did he tell you his reason ? "

" No."

" Did you ask it ? "

" No. He is a human tiger, hungry for
other men's lives, and—— "

" But he must have some reason at least
for wanting this particular man's life first."

" I don't believe he has. He knows that
the police are after James, and, as they can't
find him, he wants to show that he is cleverer
than they are ! "

It was the first time she had been rational
enough to admit James's guilt; but he took no
apparent notice of that.

" That isn't reason enough for an English
gentleman—— "

" Gentleman ! "

" Yes, Captain Morrison is a gentleman;
and, if he really is possessed with this strange
idea, he must either have, or think he has, the
very strongest of motives, or, what is more
likely, his head must be affected. Do you

know whether he ever received a wound in the head ? ”

“ Not that I have ever heard of. And you said just now he was fanatical ? ”

“ Yes ; but I did not mean that he would carry fanaticism as far as murder. What first roused your suspicions ? ”

“ When we were at Nice, I found that Sir James and Lady Otway—— ”

She hesitated and blushed, as Reginald’s attention instantly became more acute.

“ Go on, go on ! ”

“ I found that Sir James Otway had been staying at our hotel ; then, when we got to Mentone, I found that he had been—— ”

“ I beg your pardon. You said before, ‘ And Lady Otway.’ ”

“ Yes ; but she was not really his wife ; I had found that out already,” answered Geraldine, blushing again.

“ Do you know her name ? ”

“ Mrs. Farquhar.”

Reginald considered ; presently he re-marked—

“ I think I can undertake to find you a

reason now; and, though I cannot promise that the discovery will be an unmixed relief to you, it will at least prove, I think, that your husband is not inhuman, but too human. It is getting dark now; you had better let me drive you back to Waringham."

She started away from him.

He continued quietly—

"The 4.31 has gone, the next train to London is not till 6.17. You would have to wait more than an hour and a half."

"Then I will wait. I will never go back to Waringham."

"May I ask where you think of going?"

"I shall go to some hotel in London; I have plenty of money with me, and a cheque-book. And I shall go to the place where I know James is or was, and warn him."

"Allow me to say that is the most fatal thing you could do for yourself and him. Even putting aside the uncomfortable position in which, in the circumstances you have admitted, you would put yourself, nothing can be easier than for your husband to track you, who are not accomplished in the art of dodging detectives, and so to reach him, if indeed you know where he is, without further trouble."

Geraldine shuddered.

"What am I to do?" she asked earnestly, conquering a strong inclination to sit down and cry helplessly.

"You are to let me drive you back to the Hall." She instantly drew herself up in indignant protest. "Any other course is ruin to you all. How can you prevent your husband from carrying out his designs, if you cannot watch him and defeat them as they are formed?"

"And play the spy in my turn?" she faltered. It was a strong and well-urged argument nevertheless.

"You will not have much to do in that way. If you will trust me with the name of the place where James lives, I will myself try to hunt him out and warn him, on condition—I must make this condition, that you will not only remain under the same roof with your husband, but will honestly try to believe what, I assure you, you may count upon as true—that there is too much manliness, too much loyalty, in a man who has served his country with as much

distinction as Captain Morrison has, for him
to be capable of forming such a horrible design
—I must call it that—without motives the
strength of which calmer men can scarcely
measure. Now will you try to do this ? "

She was shaken, shattered by all she had
gone through lately, and by the culminating
excitement of this afternoon. She looked up
at him despairingly, waveringly. He saw his
advantage, and, speaking soothing words to her,
he led her out and helped her into the Norfolk
cart in which, six months ago, he had first
taken her to Waringham. The sight of it un-
hinged her still more ; but he would not let her
talk ; he drove fast up the sloping hill, rather
anxious about the way in which Geraldine
would satisfactorily account for this escapade.

"When did you see me ? I know you did
see me," she asked, when she had fought for
control of herself. " I thought, as I came,
I saw you on horseback, with your back to me."

"So you did," said he quietly. " I saw you
long before you saw me, and I turned up that
road so that you might think I hadn't. I knew
something was wrong by the furtive way in

which you were hurrying along—the most suspicious walk I ever saw, by-the-by—and by the mere fact of your being out alone to-day."

" But I thought you were short-sighted ? "

"Never mind ; I saw you," he went on tranquilly. " So I rode into Goldborough after you, guessing where you had gone, you see ; and made an exchange with my father, who was at the Library. I gave him the cob to ride home, and he handed over the cart to me."

It was getting dusk as they approached Waringham, and poor Geraldine began to shudder and sigh at the prospect before her.

" I am so frightened," she said in a whisper. " And, if I cry, it will be worse than ever for me ; he is always complaining of my want of spirit."

" Is he ?   Then why don't you show him a little ?   I'm sure you have plenty.   You used to treat me in a very spirited manner."

" Don't ! " she cried, drawing a sharp breath. " It is very difficult to be spirited to a person you don't like, and yet are bound to obey.   He likes dashing women," she added, after a pause.

"Then be dashing; make him like you, and persuade him to forgive James. Many women with less advantages than you have done as much."

She looked at him in astonishment.

"Oh, I couldn't, I couldn't—I hate him so!"

"I thought you owed so much to James you would do anything to serve him?"

"Yes, yes, I know; but one can't do impossibilities."

But she was thinking it over; and Reginald, who had made the proposal, not for James's sake, but for the sake of her own happiness, saw that the bait was taking. At the lodge-gates he set her down. As she held his hand to say "Good-bye," she suddenly realized what he was doing for her; she had simply told him "Enfield" as a guide to finding James, and then she said—

"Good-bye; I can't thank you. How good you are!"

"Too good, you know!" he reminded her in the same gentle voice as ever; and it was only from a slight quivering of the muscles of his face as he raised his hat to her that she guessed that he might perhaps have had feelings of his own to control while listening to the recital of her troubles.

She hurried through the park with a fast-beating heart, intent on a resolve so bold that it braced her flagging spirits and restored animation to her tired frame. She rang the bell sharply, and, passing, with head in air, the exclaiming and frightened butler, she faced her husband, who was standing, with the blackest frown she had ever seen on his face, in the hall to meet her.

CHAPTER X.

IT was a critical moment for Geraldine when, returning home after her wild attempt at flight, she found herself face to face with her husband. He was standing ready to meet her in the outer hall, his dark face lowering with anger ; his figure was so erect, his attitude so menacing, that increased stature could scarcely have given him more dignity or have inspired greater terror in his truant wife.

For a moment her spirit failed her, and she was on the point of making dutiful submission, as she had done to him before with such irritating effect, when, by good or ill fortune, he addressed her in a tone so arrogant that she was roused instantly to defiance without any further effort. He only waited until Johnson had disappeared before he said—

"Well, what account have you to give of yourself?"

She was in front of him, flushed and trembling; but at these words she suddenly raised her head, and, looking down at him through her eyelashes from the advantage in stature which her high-heeled boots gave her, she replied simply—

"I have none." And with an appearance of coolness and self-possession which the rapid beating of her heart belied, she left him and walked leisurely towards the staircase.

For a few moments Captain Morrison stood still, overcome with surprise; but before she had ascended three steps he hastened after her, and, conscious of the importance of position, passed her on the staircase, and faced her from an eminence of a couple of steps above her. She stopped, with her hand on the banisters, but did not look up.

"Am I to understand, madam," he began impressively, "that you decline to give an explanation of your extraordinary conduct this afternoon?"

"As long as you demand it in that 'stand

and deliver' fashion, I do distinctly decline to give it. When you choose to ask in a different manner, I may perhaps furnish you with the information you require."

And she raised her head and looked at him with a defiant haughtiness which was not unbecoming, while the slow emphasis with which she rolled out the dignified words she had instinctively chosen seemed to imply that she found some pleasant zest in this new and dangerous game. Captain Morrison was not a man with a particularly strong sense of humour, but he was much amused, and he took care not to hide his amusement; he leaned against the banisters and stroked his moustache in open enjoyment of her heroics, and, with a lazy look of critical admiration of the beauty of her face under this new aspect which disgusted and maddened her.

" Let me pass, if you please," she cried, with suppressed fury.

" Certainly, madam. Will you honour me with a kiss first."

" No," she promptly answered, her eyes meeting his with a look of unrepressed loathing which stung him.

She had the satisfaction of seeing the look of indolent pleasure in his eyes give place to a flash of anger. He did not attempt to take what he had asked for so unexpectedly, but, with a shrug of the shoulders and a contemptuous jerk of the head, he walked downstairs as she continued her way up. He went to the library, uttering a gruff monosyllabic laugh from time to time as he walked. When her absence had been discovered that afternoon he had been uneasy, as, in spite of the exasperating docility she had always shown to him, it occurred to him that after the scene of the night before she might have plucked up enough spirit to leave him. Such a step would have affected him very little but for the fact that the object of his marriage with her was not yet attained. Now that she had come back, he did not much care how she had employed her time away. He opened the library door so that he might hear her come down; but his anxiety to see her again arose not so much from a fear that she had been plotting, or from jealousy, as from curiosity to see whether this unaccustomed attitude of amusing defiance would

be maintained. He was not a good judge of
feminine character, and he had never made the
slightest attempt to study that of his wife. He
divided women into two classes—pretty women
who were more or less vain and silly, and were
to be kissed and indulged, and plain women,
who were sensible and good-tempered, and
therefore to be tolerated and respected. Differences of temper he admitted, differences of
taste he doubted ; but that feminine beauty and
intelligence were found in inverse proportion he
considered to be a fact beyond dispute.

Geraldine did not come down. After a
while, hearing sounds of voices and footsteps
on the floor above, he went out, listened at the
bottom of the staircase, and heard the voices of
his wife and Mrs. Symes giving orders to some
of the servants. He could hear the former
directing her maid to take her gowns and her
trunks out of the room in which they had been
put, and to be careful as she carried them along
the corridor.

"That's cool!" he muttered ; then in an
authoritative tone, he called out — "Geraldine !"

She came slowly to the banisters on the landing, looked over, and asked coldly—

"Did you call me?"

"Yes; come down here. I want to speak to you."

He doubted whether she would obey him; but she came at once, very slowly, very deliberately, giving a last injunction to Aurélie to be sure that a handsome gown of lavender brocade and gauze, which was piled up in the maid's arms, was not caught by the door-handles as it was carried along the corridor.

"What are you doing up there?" he asked, when at last she reached the bottom stair after an insolently slow descent, during which he had again watched her, not without admiration.

"I am having my things taken out of your room."

"You should have consulted me first."

She shrugged her shoulders without looking at him.

"After last night's scene, it was quite evident that you were not more likely to pine for my society than I for yours."

He stood looking at her, pulling his moustache rather savagely.

"Will you have the kindness to look at me when you are addressing me? The incivility of your speeches I can overlook, but I will not have them flung at me as if I were a servant."

With serene audacity she turned her head and returned his look with chilling steadiness. Her coldness amazed him and pained him more than she, who understood him as little as he did her, could have believed possible. He was passionate and sensitive; until to-day his own absorption in a matter which demanded all his energies, his wife's timid constraint in his society, had rendered him as indifferent to her charms as it is possible for the newly-married husband of a beautiful wife to be; but now that his interest in her was for a moment roused by her unexpected change of conduct, her open parade of dislike gave him a great shock. His own eyes shrank away under the cold gaze he had challenged; for a moment he could say nothing. Her voice, in the same hard tone, grated again on his ears.

"Is that all you have to say?"

"No, by Heaven, it is not!" he began furiously. Then, recollecting himself as he met her unflinching look again, he added, in a voice he meant to be as cold as her own, but in which it was easy for her to detect the tremor of suppressed passion, "You can go. I will speak to you again when you are in a different mood."

She gave him a curtsey which roused in him an unmanly longing to box her ears, and turned his back upon her sharply, with his right fist clenched and an unorthodox exclamation on his lips. But she had not gone two steps before he called her back again, and laying his hand almost roughly upon her shoulder, he said—

"Now tell me the truth. Where did you go this afternoon? And who did you meet? I must and will know who put you up to this unladylike, unwomanly conduct."

"Of course, if I speak at all, what I say will be the truth."

"No more airs. Go on."

She was getting rather frightened, under all her bravado, by the storm she had raised; so she spoke at once, and the fierce excitement which had enabled her to maintain that white heat which had looked like cold insensibility, now took a different form.

"I went to Goldborough ; I meant to run away. I should have run away if I had not met the man I most respect in the world, and if I had not been persuaded by him, against my better judgment, to return. As to the person who 'put me up' to running away, and who 'put me up' to having a will of my own, it is the man who married me without caring for me, to carry out a cruel, wicked purpose, the man I hate," she hissed out at him between her teeth, "as I never thought I could hate any one. Now turn me out if you like ; there is nothing in the world I wish for more."

She stood before him when she had ended, white and panting, sullen and angry, as much a contrast to the fair, modest girl he had so carelessly wooed as if she had been another woman. But to this man, who had never until the evening before guessed the depth of her feelings, she was far more attractive in her stormy defiance than she had been in her shy and almost awkward submission.

"So you hate me, do you ?" he said very

quietly, after a short pause. "Very well then. I am not going to reward you for your heartless and wicked words by letting you have your wish. You will remain under this roof, and I can promise you that you shall be troubled with as little of my society as you can possibly desire."

And he, in his turn, made her a low bow, and stalked off with what dignity he could, still in a tumult of passions, to the outer hall, where he snatched up his hat and went out to cool himself in the park.

Geraldine thought that altogether she had come off very well in the encounter, and she ran up, still trembling with excitement, and rather incoherent in the further orders she gave the servants, who were busy preparing for her use the room which had once been James's. It was tiny and inconvenient, but it was as far as possible from her husband's, and opposite to the head of the back staircase; so that she could, if she chose to go up and down in that ignominious fashion, avoid altogether the possibility of meeting her lord and master. She had obtained the key of it that morning from Miss

Elizabeth, who had never allowed it to be opened during all the six years since the news of James's conviction first came from Ireland. The dust and cobwebs of six years filled the room when Geraldine entered ; one pane of the window had got broken, and a bat flew round the walls and made her shriek before it escaped through the hole in the glass.

There was not space for much attempt at comfort in the room ; but of course Geraldine, in the indulgence of a whim, did not mind that. The bedstead which had been good enough for James was a small, folding one, which was apt to fold itself up of its own accord in the middle of the night ; that now gave place to one less active, and room was found for a small writing-table. But the dirty old birds' nests, the fir-cones, and the pet rabbit stuffed by James himself, with waistcoat-buttons for eyes, and a handsome tail which had evidently not belonged to it in life, were allowed to remain upon the mantelpiece. And the pictures of pirates and animals, torn out of books and newspapers, were left pinned to the walls of the room by its new occupant.

It was not until after dinner that evening
that Captain Morrison learnt where it was that
his wife had chosen to instal herself, and he
received the news of this caprice with grave
displeasure, to which she paid no heed. But
she had sense enough to see that some effort
was required to make the new state of affairs
between them tolerable to both; and she
adopted towards him a manner outwardly
courteous but no longer submissive.   From
the first moment of their meeting at the dinner-
table after the stormy interview in the hall, he
had been wondering what course she meant to
adopt, and was again forced to admire this
unexpected tact.   That evening his manner
was sullen, and he talked as little as usual ;
but he listened, sometimes with contempt,
sometimes with annoyance, never with absolute
indifference, to every word she spoke, though
his eyes never once turned in her direction.
In the course of the evening she expressed a
fear of being bored, and civilly asked her
husband if he had any objection to her trying
to revive, when their mourning allowed it, the
old gaieties of Waringham, and if she might

try her hand at entertaining as soon as she could. To which he replied briefly that she might entertain whom she pleased. The old ladies heard her with astonishment at the change of taste, as they thought it, which had appeared in shy, solitary Geraldine; but she laughed rather feverishly as they exchanged glances, and said—

"Ah, you think I am too ambitious; but you have only seen me under one aspect, and you don't know me yet."

The truth of this soon dawned upon them as, very gradually at first, but with the sure hand of one fitted by nature for the task, Geraldine gained the reputation of being the most charming hostess as well as the prettiest woman in that part of the county. She and Elizabeth, who was glad to see the Hall regain its lost position, cleverly met each other halfway in the difficult matter of the retiring of the elder to make way for the younger lady as mistress of the house. On the whole, young Mrs. Morrison was chary of alarming innovations; but she neglected the barouche for a neat brougham, and she insisted on the re-

furnishing of the drawing-room. Life seemed
to go on easily enough at the Hall after that
first stormy day; Geraldine threw herself
energetically into the business of receiving and
returning calls, and in superintending such re-
furnishing as she had decreed, and the filling of
the conservatory—a task in which she delighted.
She avoided being alone with her husband for
a single moment, would not even pay a call
with him without the presence of one of the old
ladies in the carriage. This of course quickly
had the result of his letting her pay them without him. This fact, and rumours of singular
domestic arrangements, gave the gossip-loving
neighbours something to talk about; but no
authentic account of a quarrel ever got abroad.
The wife's manner to her husband was charmingly deferential and good-humoured; the
husband's was less gracious certainly, but then
Captain Morrison, taciturn and gloomy, was
already looked upon as rather a bear, and if
the perfect happiness of the newly-married
couple were doubted, nobody was likely to be
sorry for him.

But, of the two, he had the worse time of

it. In the first three weeks after their return, Geraldine had plenty of occupation of a kind which pleased her. One part of her imaginative and excitable nature was satisfied with the enjoyment she managed to extract from visits and entertainments in which she was the centre of attraction ; and if, when night came and she found herself alone in her room listening to the boisterous winds which began to howl round the house in warning of the coming winter, she sobbed at the thought of the lonely life which stretched before her, and longed with a deep and wistful longing which she had never known before, which she could not understand, for some tidings of her poor brother, as in her prayers she called James, yet at least she had had some consolations, and even the fact that she could cry by herself over her grief was a solace.

But Captain Morrison found no pleasure in dinner-parties at which he generally found himself between two important be-capped and greedy dowagers with nothing to say to him and no power of inspiring him to speech, watching the beautiful woman he had married

as she sat smiling and gracious, apparently
extracting incomprehensible enjoyment from
the conversation of a pompous rural dean or a
lad fresh from Cambridge. He thought her
charming; he wondered that he had not found
it out before; and one night, when they were
returning home in the barouche, and he looked
at her as, muffled up in furs to guard her
against the piercing cold of the late October
night, she lay back with closed eyes by the side
of Miss Elizabeth—Eleanor was too delicate
to go out at night—he decided within himself
a point which he had been debating for the last
few days—that he loved her.

He was a man with whom action followed
promptly on resolution. The dim light of the
carriage-lamps, which showed him his wife's
beautiful face peeping out from the hood of her
sable cloak, showed him also that the collapsed
and crumpled condition of the heap of shawls
and cloaks which contained the other lady must
be the result of slumber; therefore, no sooner
did he feel, as he leant forward in his seat to
gaze at the still, white face opposite to him, the
blood rise to his head and a great throb of

tenderness stirring his heart, than he slid down upon his knees on the floor of the carriage, seized her right hand, which hung idly down from the loose fur sleeve, and, gently pulling down the long glove, pressed his lips to her arm. But she sat upright with a start, and snatched her arm away with an abruptness which made him regain his seat in hot anger. He could not speak, however, for these movements roused Miss Elizabeth, who woke up with a slight snort which startled her excited companions, and sleepily asked if they were home yet. When they arrived, Geraldine escaped upstairs before her husband could stop her. Having thus the night for reflection, as he did not attempt to call her back, he made up his mind to come to an understanding with her next day, to tell her that he consented to overlook the childish and whimsical manner in which she had begun her married life, but that there must be no nonsense for the future ; that he had allowed her to behave in a perfectly absurd fashion too long, and that she must make up for it by exemplary conduct now. This would put matters on to a sensible footing,

and show her that he would not suffer any more
airs. She had not chosen last night to accept
his advances as a lover; well, then, she should
submit to the prosaic authority of a husband.

He determined to make known his pleasure
to her immediately after breakfast the next
morning, during which meal he was very
fidgety.

" Geraldine," he said, in a firm voice, as
soon as they all rose, " I wish to speak to
you. Can you come into the library for a few
minutes ? "

The tone was a command ; she at once
followed him obediently, and, when he had
shut the door, waited in the most perfect
attitude of dutiful submission for him to declare his wishes. He looked at the cold face,
at the statuesque repose of the figure, and
turned away from her with all his carefully
prepared speeches forgotten and his head on
fire. However, an effort must be made.

" I want you," he began abruptly, without
looking at her again—" I want you to—to
—to see about having this chair re-covered,"
he blurted out, his eyes having fallen on

the shabby old armchair, which Geraldine's improvements had left untouched in loving memory of Sir Charles.

"Certainly," said she, without even looking surprised. But suddenly she caught her breath, her face changed, and her eyes filled with tears.

"Oh, would you mind, will it matter, if I have another chair put there instead?" she asked, in a voice now sweet and pleading. "It was—my guardian's."

"Oh, yes, of course, put any chair you like!" he agreed at once; and, seizing the opportunity her softened mood seemed to offer, he came towards her and had the pleasure of seeing her stiffen back into her former rigidity at his approach.

The sight made him feel sick; he turned sharply away with a muttered—"Confound you!" and walked back to the bureau.

"Have you anything more to say?" she asked submissively.

"Yes—that if ever a woman got better treatment than she deserved, it is you, Geraldine."

"Thank you," she said with beautiful humility, and left the room.

Then he marched up and down in restless, excited fashion, calling her all sorts of names, and full of indignant astonishment at her outrageous perversity. Half a dozen times he had his fingers upon the door-handle to go in search of her and force her to listen to reason; half a dozen times he turned back again, with indecision most unusual in him, shrinking, though he would not acknowledge the fact, from again encountering that look of cold dislike which was the weapon she had chosen to repel his overtures. After spending half the morning in this unsatisfactory fashion, he suddenly and opportunely remembered that no woman's whims were worth so much consideration on the part of a reasoning man; and, seating himself at the bureau, he plunged into his correspondence. The unworthy subject, however, continued to intrude upon his thoughts, and when, after luncheon, which passed off as usual, he started for his customary afternoon ride, he had not gone far before, his longing for her kindness getting the better of his pride,

he suddenly turned his horse's head and rode
back, resolved to proceed at once upon a more
conciliatory plan.   So, on dismounting, he
turned into the rose-corner in search of a
peace-offering ; but the very last late roses,
which had lingered on past their season in this
sheltered spot, were all dead now, and he went
round the house towards the conservatory, trying to make up a speech which should combine
dignity with tenderness.   He was still engaged
upon this effort of composition when, arriving
at the conservatory, and glancing through the
steaming panes and the thick foliage of the
plants inside, he saw a pretty picture which
sent both dignity and tenderness to the winds.

His wife had strolled through the dining-
room to show the latest additions to her
beloved collection of flowers to a visitor ; and,
standing among the bright blossoms in a gown
of black silk glittering with jet, which set off
her fair complexion and chestnut hair, she
looked handsome and, moreover, bright and
happy—a consummation which her husband,
in a passion of rage and jealousy, ascribed to
the fact that her companion was Reginald

Bamber. The young man was bending down and speaking very earnestly, and she was listening with an intent interest which gave her face both colour and animation. And the case against both, already strong in the husband's eyes, was still further strengthened when, on his opening the door and appearing at the further end of the conservatory, both started in unmistakable confusion. The greeting between the two men was rather awkward. Geraldine did not even attempt to conceal her annoyance at the interruption ; and when, after an inspection of the flowers, in which Reginald alone was able to take real interest, the latter took his leave, Mrs. Morrison had the audacity to exchange a few words with him in a very low voice in the very presence of her husband, standing a few feet away. And the words she said were—

" Write to me."

" I dare not."

" You must. Give me a note after church." She added a message to the Vicar and his wife in a louder voice, and coolly and deliberately watched him down the drive with evident interest, which was not only calculated to irritate her husband, but designed to do so.

"What were you whispering to Mr. Bamber?" asked Captain Morrison, with an unsuccessful attempt at indifference, as his wife turned from the door.

"Oh, nothing," she replied petulantly, "except a few words about flowers! If you are going to be jealous of every one I speak to, you had better employ a detective at once; you are fond of that sort of thing, I know."

And, for the first time openly disregarding his commands, she ran into the dining-room and upstairs to the top of the house, where, going through the trap-door out on to the roof, which was flat and made a very pleasant promenade, she closed the trap-door after her, and, sitting down breathless upon the edge of the parapet, she looked out over the wide landscape, her hands clasped tightly together and her face flushed with hope and excitement. She had encouraged her husband's jealousy of handsome Reginald Bamber in order to prevent his suspecting the real reason of the interest she took in his society. At the moment when her hus-

band's appearance in the conservatory broke
off their conversation, he had just told her
that he had been to Enfield, and had been
successful in finding a clue to James Otway's
present hiding-place. More she must know.
Badly as James had behaved, her old affection
and pity for him had sprung up again in the
faithful heart of the woman, and no reproach
she could find for him was so strong as that
she made to herself for having allowed herself
for one moment to forget the gratitude which,
in spite of all his faults, she romantically believed she owed him.

She was so hopeful, so happy, that, when
she descended from her retreat and met her
husband, still looking angry and sullen, at the
drawing-room door, she made submission very
sweetly, and turned aside the torrent of his
displeasure by a gaiety which charmed while
it disquieted him. For he felt that this en-
viable self-possession was a suspicious quality,
and that, if she could only be light-hearted as
the result of another man's society, he would
prefer that she should not be light-hearted at all.
However, he had no opportunity of saying

this, and both husband and wife walked safely on the volcano until the following day, which was Sunday. In the morning, after church, Geraldine devoted herself, outside the little porch, to the Vicar and his family, was solicitous about the effects of the recent fogs on Mrs. Bamber's throat, was anxious to hear the latest tidings of the boys at Shrewsbury; but her husband shared her interest in these and kindred subjects with such keenness that it was impossible for her to exchange a word with Reginald unheard by him.

" Is there an afternoon-service here to-day? " she asked carelessly, before the group broke up.

" No, not here—at Cawfield," said Reginald.

And her eyes rested for just one moment longer on his face, with an intimation which he understood.

Five minutes after she had retired that afternoon to her own room, with two three-volume novels " to choose from," she had slipped out of the house, and on her way through the grass-walk bound for Cawfield Church. In the state of unnatural and un-

healthy excitement which she now habitually
encouraged as her best refuge from the exagge-
rated horror she took of her position as the
wife of a man she disliked, these little shifts
and subterfuges to trick him and escape him
amused her; and she fled through the wood
with light steps, her cheeks burning with
triumph at having outwitted him. As her
trembling fingers lifted the latch of the side
gate at the end of the wood-path, she gave one
look behind her as she fancied she heard the
crackling of a branch; but she was not pursued; and, turning again, she slipped through
the gate, and was shutting it behind her, when
she caught sight of her husband, leaning against
a gate on the other side of the road about fifty
yards away. He had a cigar between his lips,
and his hands in his pockets, and his head was
turned away from her; but she knew that he
was on the watch, and felt also that her guilty
start did not escape him. After one moment
of hesitation her spirit rose, and she walked on
in his direction, and was passing him with a
most hypocritical smile when he came up to
her, with a manner which was meant to be as
sweet as her own.

"Going to church twice in one day!" he exclaimed, with badly acted surprise which disgusted her, though his duplicity was certainly no deeper than her own.

"Yes. But I own I expect to enjoy the walk more than the sermon."

"Will it spoil the pleasure if I come with you?" he asked, with what seemed to her hideous amiability.

"On the contrary. Of course I shall enjoy it much more," she answered, with effrontery which cut him to the heart, while it inflamed his anger still more against her.

He wanted to speak seriously to her, he wanted to bully her, he longed to make love to her; but she would chatter the lightest of talk about the fields and the fogs and the coming week's arrangements, and, as her heart was free and her head cool, all the advantage was on her side, and she had her way with the talk for the whole two miles until they reached the straggling cluster of houses, in the midst of which stood Cawfield Church. The absurdity of any one not belonging to the parish coming to listen to the curtailed service, which was a

race between parson and clerk, in which most
of the congregation fell out very soon, and to
the musty old college sermon, too pedantically
worded for an ordinary congregation, which the
Rev. Albert Thorpe found good enough for
a handful of villagers, was so apparent that the
appearance of Captain and Mrs. Morrison sat
everybody whispering ; and when, just as the
harmonium had gasped out the last wheezy note
of the voluntary, young Mr. Bamber came in
and shut himself modestly into a pew as near
as he could to the door, nobody scrupled to
stare at him open-mouthed and to wag his
head at his neighbour in a way which implied
the general opinion that the gentry were odd
folk.

The Rev. Albert Thorpe took the honour of
the visit to himself, and divided his attentions
between them, addressing the prayers and
thanksgivings to the Vicar's son, thundering out
the Commandments straight at Captain Morrison,
and reserving the well-rounded and sonorous
periods of his sermon for Geraldine. When
service was over, and Mr. Thorpe had hurried
out of the old-fashioned three-decker, which

was pulpit and lectern for him and desk for the clerk, and had retired behind a sheet hung up in the corner to take off his surplice, Reginald waited at the church door for his neighbours, and they all three walked back to Waringham together, after having duly congratulated Mr. Thorpe, who rushed out for the purpose, and who begged young Mr. Bamber to ask the Vicar to tell Wilkins to let him have better candles in the pulpit. The clerk would put tallow ones, and Mr. Thorpe complained that they grew so dim for want of snuffing that he could not see to read, and it was unseemly for a minister of the Gospel to have to stop in the middle of his discourse to snuff them with his fingers.

Talk was kept up easily enough until they all three, having parted with Mr. Thorpe at the turning which led to the farmhouse where he had tea on these occasions, reached the side gate which opened into the wood in Waringham Park. It was getting dark and foggy, and, as Reginald, on shaking hands with Geraldine, slipped a note from his hand into hers, both flattered themselves that the action was unseen. As a matter of fact they were right; but Captain Morrison's suspicions were so fully roused that the fact that his wife appeared perfectly contented and even gay on her way through the wood to the house with him, seemed to his jealous mind sufficient proof that she had found some means of communicating secretly with Reginald Bamber under his very nose. So that, on arriving at the house, he followed her into the drawing-room, where she went at once to avert suspicion that she was in haste to be alone; and, turning up the lamp high, while his dark eyes burnt with a fierceness which frightened her, he said shortly—

" Now, the letter! Give me the letter ! "

No acting was proof against such a surprise as that; the flash of terror over her face, the involuntary step back were enough for him. The low sound which escaped between his teeth as he leant over the table and glared at her with clenched fists and dark, livid face, seemed to the horror-struck woman like the cry of a savage animal. She tried to laugh, but her ease was gone: with that letter, which contained, as she knew, the means of setting this man with his blood-hound ferocity straight upon the track of a man she loved in her pocket, she felt for the moment numb, power-less, lost.   She could only stand and watch the horrible convulsive quivering of his face, with-out thought, without feeling.   It was only a few moments, but it seemed to her a very long time before he spoke again.

" The letter !   Make haste.   Give it me."

Life and thought were coming back to her ; simple feminine instinct suggested the first in-evitable shuffling speech—

" Letter !   What letter ? "

It added fuel to the fire which was raging in the man's veins.

" Confound your prevarication.   Don't you see that you are found out, that you are caught, that the best thing you can do for yourself is to confess, to throw yourself on my mercy ? "

Mercy !   Wiser   to   hope   for   it   from   a wounded tiger, from a famished blood-hound than from this man !

" What am I to confess ?   What have you found out ? "

A second pause—during which he saw a

light pass over her face ; the next moment her
hand stole to her pocket. He was watching
her intently, not a movement could escape
him. He saw the fingers fumble, disappear,
reappear—clutching something he could not
yet see. But he knew what it was, and he slid
a step farther towards her round the table. As
he did so, she sprang across the hearthrug, and
thrust the letter through the bars of the grate
into the red heart of the fire. He was coming ;
he was upon her ; but before he could push her
aside she had sprung erect, faced him, and flung
her arms round him to detain him till the last
scrap of the paper was consumed. For the
moment her touch seemed to paralyze him, he
could not fling her aside ; then, his fury rising
again, he put up his hands to free himself from
hers, which she had clasped at the back of his
neck. But when his fingers touched hers, his
face changed ; his hands fell to his sides, he
shook from head to foot, and, laying his head
on her shoulder, he whispered hoarsely—

"Oh, Heaven, what have you done to me?"

But the paper was burnt, by turning her
head she could see that ; and, freeing herself

with a sob of relief, she met his eyes as he
raised his head sharply.   But the agony which
had replaced the anger in his face she did not
understand.

" Now, what have you got to ask ?   What
have you to say ?   You want to know what the
letter said, I suppose, or do you——"

He interrupted the stream of her feverish,
querulous questions in a low, monotonous,
almost weak voice, which made her look at
him more attentively.

" No.   I don't want to know—anything
more.   You can—leave me."

He was leaning against the mantelpiece,
which his shoulders only just reached, almost
as if he wanted its support ; his dark face was
very pale, and he seemed to be breathing with
some difficulty.

" Are you—are you not well, Philip ? " she
asked uncertainly, coming a step nearer.

" I am not in need of your assistance, thank
you."

He spoke coldly, not rudely ; and she went
without another word, somewhat crestfallen,
somewhat hurriedly, towards the door.   But

just as she reached it, and when the partition
hid her from his sight, a moan broke upon her
ears which caused her to start, and to turn, and
to put her hand slowly into her pocket and feel
for something there with trembling fingers, and
doubt in her eyes. But in another moment she
heard an impatient movement and a curse from
her husband's lips ; and, dropping again into
her pocket that which she had half withdrawn,
she opened the door and slipped through and
shut it in nervous haste, and, hurrying up to
her own room like a hare, locked herself in with
a great sigh of ease from her burden.

For she had tricked him after all.

CHAPTER XI.

THE candles in Geraldine's room had already been lighted by her maid, and she watched them flickering in the gust her flying entrance had caused, listening in dread lest her husband's suspicions should bring him to her door, in which case that frail wooden structure would scarcely stand long in his way. In a few minutes her groundless fears subsided, and, drawing from her pocket the note which Reginald had given her, in place of which she had thrown into the fire a letter from Miss Gretton which she had suddenly remembered she had about her, she opened it very softly, lest the mere rustle of paper should fall on listening ears, and read it almost without daring to draw breath.

" DEAR MRS. MORRISON,

"I am sorry to have to communicate
with you in this manner, as, if it should in any
unforeseen way come to your husband's knowledge, it would naturally annoy him very much.
However, if I am unable to give you the tidings
you wish for by word of mouth, as you seem to
fear will be the case, this note will inform you
that I have been to the place you mentioned,
and have learnt that the person about whom
you are anxious does not go there, but that a
man named Hammond has made two brief
visits there within the month of September.
I think it probable that he was a friend or
agent of the other. The man Hammond, on
one of his two visits, ordered some things of a
local tradesman for the use of the person he
was visiting, and ordered that the bill should be
sent to an address which duly found him—' No.
5, Bankside Cottages, Chiswick.' I don't know
whether you will consider this much of a clue,
or whether you will decide to make any use of
it. If so, I hope you will be cautious. The
man may be—probably is—a rogue; and I
think, harsh as it may sound to say so, the

better as well as the wiser course for you to pursue now would be to reconcile yourself to circumstances, and leave a man who, you must own, shows considerable ability in keeping out of the way of well-merited punishment, to his fate.

"Perhaps you will forgive my presumption in offering you advice, in consideration of the alacrity I have shown in obtaining for you the information you desired.

"Yours very truly,

"REGINALD D. BAMBER."

Geraldine read this letter three times, and then she held it in one of the candles until it was totally destroyed, and, opening the window, she let the black, brittle remains of the paper be carried away in morsels by the wind. There was no fear of her forgetting one syllable of the information it had given her, and it was too dangerous a document to be allowed to remain in existence. Then she sat down, glancing at her little clock as she did so. They dined an hour earlier on Sunday; it was six o'clock, she had only half an hour before her in which to decide upon a line of conduct to be pursued towards her husband, in order to attain her object of going to London without him. No letter would serve her purpose ; she must see this man Hammond, make her own observations as to whether he were worthy of trust, and try to discover from him where James was and whether he was safe and well. After a struggle between reason and her affectionate instincts, Geraldine's belief in his innocence had risen again triumphant; and imagination, which was her strongest faculty, persisted in picturing him as the victim of some plot whose nature she guessed at continually, but could not determine. A month ago, the assurance of some person such as Reginald Bamber, in whom she could trust, would have satisfied her of the exile's safety ; but ever since the discovery of her husband's designs upon him, her own solicitude had grown so rapidly, he was so continually in her thoughts and even in her dreams, that she felt that nothing but the evidence of her own eyes could content her ; she must see him, and soon. Now and then a horrible fear would cross her mind that he was dead, perhaps killed by her husband, of whose anxiety to find him she had heard no more since the night of their arrival at Waringham. The fear struck her with fresh force now, paralyzed her, and took away her power of thought. When the dinner-bell rang she went downstairs, pale, anxious-looking, undecided. She and her husband watched each other furtively during the meal, which was short and silent. As soon afterwards as she could, Geraldine stole away from the drawing-room to the conservatory, and, throwing herself into an American chair which stood in a corner surrounded by some of her favourite friends among the flowers, she closed her eyes and tried to arrange her feverish imaginings into connected thoughts.

The dim light from the fantastic Chinese lanterns with which it was her pleasure that her fairy-land should be lighted, struggled through the thick, tinted glass, the grotesque figures on which threw distorted shadows on the stone floor and on her own face and figure as she lay back in nervous unrest, with one hand raised to her hot and aching head. The perfume of a cigar caused her to open her eyes to see the dark figure of her husband standing a few steps from her among the flowers, the demon in her paradise.

" I did not mean to disturb you," he apologized, stepping back as he noted the too eloquent expression of her face. " I did not know you were here."

" Pray don't go," said she civilly, ashamed of her unguarded expression of dislike.

And it suddenly occurred to her that there was something pitiful in the way in which he slunk back to the door, turned away from the enjoyment of the pretty things he had provided for her by her own ungraciousness. She put pressure upon herself, and, hurrying after him, laid her hand upon his shoulder.

" You know I don't mind the scent of a cigar at all, Philip," she said, gently.

He turned his head and looked at her with something of the pleading expression of a dog in his long, full, brown eyes.

" No ; but you mind my presence, don't you ? "

" No, I don't," she answered impatiently, petulant because of the truth of the accusation.

"Come back and finish your cigar. It was all nonsense this afternoon, you know," she added hurriedly, as he yielded, half against his will, to her rather awkwardly exercised seductions, and returned towards the carpeted corner where she had been sitting. "There is not the least reason for you—for any jealousy of Mr. Bamber, and I give you my word of honour there was nothing at all affectionate in his note."

"Then why were you so anxious about it? Why any need of a note at all?"

"That was your fault. You watched me, and I won't be watched. I shouldn't care if Mr. Bamber were to go to America to-morrow."

He looked at her steadfastly, and believed, because he wanted to believe. But, if there was truth in her face, as he was inclined to think, there was no love.

"After all, what can it matter to me whether you do or do not care for another man's society as long as it is certain you can't endure mine?"

Geraldine moved restlessly; it was impossible to contradict such a truism; but something must be said to mitigate its crudity.

"Of course—of course married people can
never get on so well until—until they are used
to each other," said she, as hopefully as she
could.

"Do you think we are going the right way
to—to get used to each other?"

He had thrown away his cigar, having
burnt his fingers with it in his agitation. She
was in terror lest he should approach her,
underrating as she did the sensitiveness of the
man's nature and the quickness of his percep-
tions. How could he dare to expect wifely
duty and love from her now that she had found
out the horrible motive of his marriage with
her? But she did not want to re-open the
subject with another sense of useless, wearing
passion. She shrugged her shoulders and
turned to play with the fronds of a delicate fern.

"Well, you will soon be relieved from my
presence for a little while," he informed her
rather bitterly. "I am going to accept an invitation I had yesterday to go down to Melton
for a week's hunting. Do you think you will
be able to find some sort of a welcome for me
by the time I come back?"

The question was half a sneer; but the news fulfilled her own wishes so marvellously that there was quite a genuine ring in his wife's answer.

"I am sure I shall, Philip. I wish for your sake Norfolk were a hunting county; you will find it dull to come back to your afternoon rides."

"I should not, if——" he began impulsively, and stopped.

"If what?" she inquired, guessing what was coming, at the same moment that a scheme for carrying out her own wishes occurred to her and gave sudden brightness to her face.

"If—if you would ride with me," he replied in a hesitating voice.

"I have never learnt to ride," she answered readily. "But I think I should like it, if I were not afraid of appearing awkward at first."

"You would soon get over that. I would teach you with pleasure."

He was trying not to appear too eager. So was she, for a different reason.

"I should have to overcome the first difficulties of it before I dared to try your patience

so much," said she nervously. " I—I wish
there were a riding-school in Goldborough ;
then I would begin while you were away."

" I would give up Melton if you are really
so anxious to begin at once."

" Oh, no, no!" said she promptly, for this
was by no means what she wanted. " I would
not have you make such a sacrifice for the
world ! "

This amiability was rather excessive, and
Captain Morrison shot a keen look at her out
of his jealous eyes. She continued—

" It is your witnessing my first attempts
that I want to avoid. Isn't there some riding-
school you know of where I could be broken
in a little before coming to you for finishing
lessons ? I should not mind going up to town
for a day or two, if Miss Elizabeth would go
with me. I know I could learn there; and I
should like the change and the excitement."

This was evident enough. Her eyes were
glittering, her cheeks were flushed, she looked
eager, and even anxious. Her husband, on the
other hand, had grown very quiet, very still—
suspiciously so, she might have thought, had

she not been somewhat blinded by her own excitement and the effort to keep it in check.

"Yes," said he musingly; " you might do that certainly. When do you propose to go?"

"I don't propose at all. It is for you to make known your intentions and wishes," said she gaily.

"You seem very much pleased at the idea of going away."

"I am—I own it. I have seen scarcely anything of London; and what I have seen I love."

She was looking so radiant, so lovely in her delight at having gained her point that he was irresistibly drawn a step nearer to her; and he bent down over a flower to bring his head closer yet to the spot where her little white fingers were playing with the leaves of a plant.

"Why didn't you tell me so before? I would have taken a house in town for you. You shall have one there next season, if you like."

"Oh, well, we can talk about that later on!" almost gasped Geraldine, upon whose ears the suggestion of a perpetual *tête-à-tête* with her husband fell with appalling suddenness.

"Yes, of course; anything that concerns me and my happiness can be shelved till later on," said he, with a warning growl in his voice which snuffed out her exultation in a moment.

She was rather sorry for this man now and then, with his fierce, concealed passions, which seemed to make his own life a burden to him; but she feared him, and the moment his passions threatened to emerge from their concealment she hated him.

"I didn't know that you were fond of London, indeed," said she, with the deadened, spiritless meekness which always exasperated him.

"You don't care what I'm fond of, as long as it is something that keeps me out of your way, do you? Your husband's affections are no concern of yours."

"A wife married as I was married cannot expect affection."

"And does not wish for it?"

Her spirit rose, and, facing him, she echoed his words—

" And does not wish for it."

"Great Heavens! You can say that to my face?"

" Why not? Is it such an astounding thing that a woman you married simply that she might become the unconscious accomplice in the murder of her brother should not bear you the love of a wife won for herself?"

" Even if it were as you say, that would be no concern of yours. All that a wife has a right to demand of her husband is that he should keep her in comfort to the best of his ability, and treat her with kindness. If every wife were to claim the right to dole out her love and duty according to the measure of approval she thought fit to bestow on her husband's general conduct, there would be no more marriages."

" It is a pity you did not explain to me your singular code before marriage; it would have saved a great deal of misunderstanding. The wife may not even claim fidelity, I see."

" Not as a right, certainly."

" Ah, your teaching is charmingly simple! Then, if she should find that in the very first

days of marriage her husband is always looking
at another woman's portrait, if 'Maud's' letters
and 'Maud's' hair are stowed away as his most
treasured possessions, the wife is to fold her
hands meekly and to submit to his neglect, his
indifference, and to be quite overwhelmed with
dutiful joy when these give place to a capricious
fancy for her."

Captain Morrison started at her mention of
the name "Maud"; but he seemed neither
confused nor displeased, but rather elated by
this sign of jealousy.

"That would be pattern conduct, certainly ;
but, fortunately for you, I happen to admire
spirit in a woman, or I should not submit to
your living under my roof on the terms you
have chosen."

"You know that on any other terms I
should not live here at all."

"You cannot suppose I shall allow your
absurd arrangement to be permanent ?"

"It will be until you are tired of the sight
of me.   Yes," she flashed out with passion, "if
you hid a cruel secret from me, I hid something
fiercer in me than what you call 'spirit' from

you. But your deception was wilful, and mine was not. I was never badly treated before, so that I did not know how strong my instincts of justice and resistance were. You should not have married the daughter of a peasant if you wanted a pretty little puppet for your wife!"

"Perhaps I knew what I wanted better than you think," said he, quietly.

"So you overhauled my letters? At least I can hardly say that, for apparently you did not read them. You cannot have been very jealous!"

"I did not care enough."

"So I see. Maud is—was—my sister."

"Your sister!"

"Yes, I would have told you before, if you had asked me; but, as you say, you did not care; besides, the story concerned another person. As you have proved your claim to be more than a puppet, you can hear it now." He was speaking with extraordinary quietness, the quietness of severe self-repression, and he went on in a low, monotonous voice—"She was a girl of 'spirit,' and I dare say it was because I worshipped her so, and thought that there was

nobody like her, that I never fell very deeply
in love, never lost my head about a woman
until recently—quite recently. While I was
away on service in India, she married, threw
herself away, I thought, on a man old enough
to be her father. He was very rich, and I
suppose she thought she would be able to do
what she liked with him. However, it turned
out that he was a jealous and intractable old
brute, and he took her away to live in an out-
of-the-way place of his in Somersetshire—
almost shut her up, in fact. I had been ordered
home, and was looking forward to seeing her,
and determined to go down and remonstrate
with her husband, when suddenly came like a
thunderbolt upon me the news that she had
left him—with another man." Geraldine was
listening, horror-struck, spell-bound, guessing
the sequel. "I need not tell you what oath I
swore—perhaps you can guess, perhaps you
can understand. I reached England, learned
they had gone abroad. I would set no vulgar
detective to the wretched task which was the
one object of my life now. I knew the name of
the man I was pursuing ; I found out his home ;

I settled myself there to watch like a terrier for a rat. No means were too ignoble for me, no course was too daring. I met a person who would, I knew, sooner or later, be able to give me a clue—if she would—at last I felt sure she had got it; but by that time I knew that, as an acquaintance—as a friend, she would never trust me with it. I determined to acquire the only right which would enable me to get it."

"But you failed, and you will always fail. You have sacrificed me—and yourself, to no purpose. Your love for your sister cannot possibly be greater than mine for my adopted brother; and I warn you that, should you ever, in spite of my utmost efforts, get on his track and hunt him down, I will never live to be the wife of his murderer. On the day that you lift your hand against James Otway, you will be free to try your matrimonial code on some meeker woman than I ?"

Husband and wife stood facing each other, will opposed to will, eye flashing into eye, both very quiet, the self-control of each affecting the other; and both, at the moment of their mutual defiance, admiring each other more than they had ever done before. But Geraldine's was only the admiration of sudden respect added to fear; in her husband it was the spark that kindled his passion into flame.

He drew nearer to her, stirred as no woman's fairness had stirred him, by her beauty, animated as it was by the qualities he most admired, by steadfast loyalty and fearless daring.

"Geraldine," said he in a hoarse voice, as he crept towards her, his dark face pallid and his dark eyes burning in weird contrast which made him look diabolical in the eyes of the woman he was approaching, "I want no meek woman, I want you. I love you!"

She shrank back without taking her eyes off his quivering, livid face, which had the fascination of horror for her. When he flung his arm round her, she only shuddered and stood passive, while he whispered into her ear with hot lips which almost touched it—

"Be kind to me, only look at me kindly, and I will worship you as no wife was ever worshipped before. See how gentle I can be! Why are you afraid of me?"

She felt like a girl in a fairy-tale in the power of a demon, for through her husband's passionate whispers she could think of nothing but that he had sworn to kill James.

"You said you would kill him!" said she faintly, not struggling but shivering at his touch.

"Oh, Geraldine, I have sworn— My honour! He is a scoundrel—why do you care?"

She wrenched herself away from him without answer. And he buried his face in his hands, shaking from head to foot in the struggle between his oath and his passion. In a few moments he started into sudden self-control, and, without looking at his wife again, walked with heavy tread towards the dining-room. But she, with a frightened guess at the nature of that debate with itself and its issue, called him back as he had his foot upon the threshold.

"Philip!" said she in a whisper.

And he wavered and stopped.

"How can you be so hard, so unchristian, so cruel?"

" I hard, cruel ! Great Heaven ! Then what are you ? "

She looked astonished in her turn—her husband came slowly back towards her.

" Listen, Geraldine ! An oath may mean nothing to a woman ; but it is a bond to me. But I will give it up, as I would give up my soul, for you to love me. Draw my head into your arms now, look into my eyes with one kind look, and kiss my lips with one kind word, and I will give up my revenge for ever."

He had drawn nearer and nearer to her, as she stood, now tearful and trembling, her figure drooping, her face softened, among the flowers. But, after the fearful excitement of the past half-hour, she was no longer capable either of consummate acting or of perfect self-control. She made one strong effort ; taking a step forward, she encircled his bent head with her trembling arms, said—

" Thank you, Philip "—with a quivering smile, and stooped to kiss him. But at the moment her lips touched his an uncontrollable shudder passed over her, and he shook her off with a hissing, deep-drawn breath, and looked at her furiously as she stood humiliated before him.

" You have saved my oath, at any rate!" said he very quietly ; and he turned and left her.

And, without a word or cry, she sank, fainting, on the stone floor.

CHAPTER XII.

IT was the French maid Aurélie who, when nine o'clock struck and her mistress did not ring for her as usual when there were no visitors in the house, went in search of madame and found her just raising herself from the conservatory floor, cold, stiff, and giddy.

When it came to Captain Morrison's ears through Elizabeth, who heard it from Aurélie, that his wife had been found lying alone in the gloom and the cold, his remorse knew no bounds. He went up to the door of her room and asked if he might see her; but she begged him to excuse her until the following day in such a frightened, broken voice, that, irritated again by her show of fear, he answered—

" All right," with sharpness which disgusted even Elizabeth, who could hear the colloquy from her room, and marched straight down-stairs to the library. And next day he made no reference to the evening's event, though a slight flush rose to his dark face on noticing, when his wife first appeared at breakfast, that she looked pale and heavy-eyed. In truth he need not have felt so conscience-stricken, for the ravages which a wakeful night had made in her looks were not due so much to his cruelty as to her anxiety on behalf of another man.

Engagements for luncheon, for dinner, calls to make and to receive, luckily gave Geraldine occupation for the first half of the week ; but the constraint between her and her husband grew daily more irksome to her, more unen-durable to him, and she heard on the Wednes-day evening, with a heart-throb of relief, that he should start for Melton the next day.

" Do you still think of going up to town to take riding-lessons ? " he asked, without looking at her.

" Yes, I think I may as well. It will give me a new occupation."

" Then I will give you an address, and I will telegraph for rooms for you and Miss

Elizabeth at a quiet hotel. How long do you propose to stay ? "

" Oh, I don't know ! I think a week, if you don't mind ; you are going to stay a week at Melton, are you not ? You might come to bring us back, and we might go to a theatre or two first. Would that suit you ? "

" Certainly. You will want some money to spend, won't you ? I will draw you a cheque."

He gave her the cheque before the evening was over ; it was for such a large sum that she begged him not to trust her with so much money.

" You know what a spendthrift I am," said she. " If you were to give me a thousand instead of a hundred, it would all slip through my fingers in the same way."

" But the spending gives you pleasure, Well, then, spend it. Since I cannot give you happiness, let my money give you a poor imitation of it."

Geraldine tore the paper, with a slight but unmistakable stamp of her foot at the same time.

" That is mean, not generous," she said.

"You want to make me feel like a fraudulent dependent."

"Not fraudulent, for I gave it to you ; and not dependent, since you have money of your own.   However, it is satisfactory to see that I can make you feel something, if it is only irritation at my ostentation."

She watched him uncomfortably as he picked up the pieces of the torn cheque and left the room.   When he returned, he did not speak to her, but spent the evening morosely over the papers ; it was not until she wished him good night that he handed her an envelope containing notes to half the amount of the cheque, and asked—

"Is that too munificent ?"

"Thank you.   It is too much, but—thank you."

The old ladies had passed out with their candles, and husband and wife were alone together.

"I shall start to-morrow, before you are up," he said, in the monotonous voice which she now knew to be a sign of a storm within.   "I will say good-bye to you now.   I have written for rooms for you at Smith's Hotel. I hope you will enjoy the change."

His eyes, too passionate at the moment to be very penetrating, were fixed upon her face, eloquent with inquiry, suspicion, and entreaty. She must act now, for some one else's sake.

" I think I shall ; it will not be your fault if I do not," she replied smiling. " You have taken every care to make it pleasant for me. Thank you."

She held her face towards him, and he accepted the invitation with fervour which caused each kiss to sting the conscience-stricken wife.

" You don't love me, I know you don't love me," he whispered huskily, as he still held her passive form in his arms. " But tell me this, on your honour, before Heaven—do you love another man ? "

" In the sense you mean, before Heaven I do not."

He understood her, and, reading truth in her eyes, he let her go, half satisfied. And he was right, for her answer was honest—her love for James was that of a sister for a fallen brother, and she had no fear that her heart would ever be stirred by a deeper passion for any man.

Next morning when she came down to breakfast, her husband—in spite of herself, to her relief—was gone. Full of the excitement which was now her only happiness, she fluttered from room to room, busy with preparations for her own departure ; and when, later in the day, she and Elizabeth and Aurélie started, it needed all her self-control to hide the fact that something of more interest than riding-lessons was the reason for her mad anxiety to go to town.

As she did not care what suspicions she might rouse, if only she could get her difficult and dangerous business over before her husband could hear of her mysterious proceedings, the very next morning she left the hotel alone, and, watching carefully to be sure that she was not followed, she walked a little way before she got into a hansom and told the man to drive to Waterloo station, having consulted "Bradshaw" the night before, and found particulars of the train to Chiswick. When he asked—"Main line or loop line, ma'am?" she began to feel

nervous, because, in her ignorance, she had to
tell him she wanted to go to Chiswick. However, it was not likely that he would be able to
make dangerous use of this information, and
there was no help for it. She caught a train
which left London at five minutes past twelve,
and reached Chiswick at twenty-three minutes
past. She asked at the station for Bankside
Cottages, and was directed to a row of small
houses facing the river. In summer-time most
of them were let in lodgings to rowing-men,
city clerks, young stock-brokers and the like ;
but now, in winter, with dead creepers hanging
like huge cobwebs on the dirty walls, they
looked damp, deserted, and inexpressibly
dreary. Mr. Hammond, whether rogue or
honest man, showed singular taste in his
choice of a residence.

Geraldine found No. 5. It seemed to
her to look drearier, more desolate than
the rest. A green stain spread from the end
of a broken water-pipe over one side of the
dingy brick front of the house, and a great
bush of untidy ivy straggled across the other
side and hung over the lower window. The

bell was broken—she went through the half-open gate, along eight or ten feet of barren garden, up the short flight of ill-kept steps, and knocked at the door. After waiting some minutes, she knocked again, and a dirty, sullen-looking woman opened the door. Geraldine wondered whether this was Mrs. Hammond.

"Does Mr. Hammond live here?" she asked, with as much assurance as she could muster.

"Which Mr. Hammond do you want?"

Geraldine was bewildered; the possibility of having to face a whole family had not occurred to her. She was about most injudiciously to ask how many Mr. Hammonds there were, when the woman continued impatiently, examining her at the same time from head to foot with evident suspicion—

"Mr. Hammond is out."

And she was on the point of shutting the door in the very face of her inquirer, when Geraldine said quietly—

"I will see the other one—the one who is in."

"Mr. Harry?"

"Yes," answered Geraldine, promptly, "Mr. Harry is the one I want."

She remembered the name on the back of the photograph.

"I don't think he's well enough to see anybody," said the woman doubtfully.

"Is he ill, then?" asked Geraldine.

"Well, it's an illness with him," answered the woman, with a wink and a gesture to intimate that the malady in question was the consequence of excess.

Geraldine shrank back as the woman stood aside to let her enter.

"Oh, you needn't be afraid!" said she, having perhaps grown a little curious as to the lady's business. "He isn't raving, or anything of that sort. He's only stupid, and perhaps you'll have a difficulty in making him understand. You needn't be frightened; I shan't be far off."

Geraldine had no doubt of that. The task before her seemed to promise to be anything but pleasant or easy; but she must go through with it now. It suddenly occurred to her that it might perhaps be easier to find out what she wanted to know concerning James from a man half-drunk than from one in the full and sober possession of his senses. So she walked resolutely into the passage, while the woman knocked at the first door on the right, and, receiving no answer, turned the handle and put her head into the room.

" Are you there, Mr. Harry? Are you awake? " She had gone in, and her voice sounded as if she was in the act of shaking him. " Here's a lady want's to see you, do you hear? A lady! "

A man's voice grunted, heaved a deep sigh, muttered something almost inarticulately.

" Here, get up; come and sit here; don't go to sleep again. Here are your boots; I'll help you on with them. Let me open the window."

There was a sound of a window being pushed open; the next moment Geraldine heard a heavy shuffling tread across the floor, and the window was slammed violently down again, with another growl in the man's voice.

" Well, I never! I never knew such a one to be afraid of a breath of fresh air. The place isn't fit to come into ; it's stifling—that's what it is."

She retreated, returning to Geraldine in the passage. But the courage of the latter had given way.

"When will the other Mr. Hammond be in ?" she asked, with trembling lips.

"The doctor ? Oh, he won't be in not before five or six—perhaps not then. He doesn't live here, you know—only comes to see his brother. He was here all last night playing cards with him up to seven o'clock this morning—not the best way to cure him, as I made bold to tell him ; but he said his brother was dull down here, and he's that fond of him that, though he don't care for cards himself, he sat up just to liven him up a bit. He's a real devoted brother, and Master Harry here"—jerking her head in the direction of the room—"he's not worth such devotion, that's my opinion. So he's not been to bed at all ; he's just been sleeping on the sofa."

"Well, I—I don't think I'll see him this morning ; I don't think it would be of much use———"

She was interrupted by a voice from the room, calling, " Mrs. Hicks ! "

Geraldine started violently, and, gasping for breath, stopped the landlady as the latter was about to enter the room.

" I'll go ; I may as well see him," she whispered hurriedly ; and, opening the door, she found herself in a rather small front sitting-room, divided by half-open folding-doors from a similar one at the back. The air was close and heavy, the window, obscured by the tangle of ivy hanging over it, let in but little light ; a small fire burning in the grate increased the oppression of the atmosphere. In an arm-chair drawn up to the hearth-rug sat a man with his back to the window ; his head was sunk upon his breast and his eyes were closed. He did not look up as Geraldine, after closing the door with trembling hands, crept nearer and nearer to him, until, stretching out one hand, she touched one of his, which was hanging list-lessly over the arm of his chair.

" James ! " she whispered faintly.

He raised his head, opened his eyes stupidly, and stared at her. She sank on her knees in

front of him, and took his nerveless hand in her
warm, quivering fingers.

"Don't you know me, James?"

His hand quivered in hers, a glimmer of
light came into his dull eyes, and burst into full
recognition as he started forward in his chair
and put his other hand upon her shoulder.

"Geraldine, Geraldine!" he cried doubtfully,
inquiringly. "Is it really you?"

"Why, yes, can't you see that it is?" she
replied, in an unsteady voice. "You can't see
me very well, certainly; but don't you know
my voice? Have you forgotten your little
sister so utterly as that? Feel."

She raised his hand lovingly to her cheek,
trying to smile at him through the tears that
would rise; but she shivered as his fingers
touched her face.

"How cold you are!" she whispered,
frightened. "You are not well, you are really
ill! Oh, what have you done to yourself?"
She rose from her knees, staring into his face
with fiercely eager scrutiny. Then her voice
changed, and she said slowly, "What have they
done to you?"

For a suspicion that her husband had been at work in some mysterious way to bring him to this condition shot through her mind as she noted the signs of a great change in him.

"Nothing," he answered, staring up at the ceiling, as he shook his head, as if trying to free himself from the cloud which still seemed to obscure his faculties. "Nobody has done anything to me, Deldee. I'm all right."

"Get up then. Come to the light; let me look at you."

He got up at her touch of command, like a man in a dream; she still held his hand in hers, and now drew him impatiently, imperiously towards the window. But he staggered as he followed her. There were two horse-hair-covered chairs there, and she made him sit down on one of them while she opened the window. He shivered again, but she was remorseless; the November fog creeping up from the river, whose cold, gray waters were visible from where she stood, could not, she was sure, do him so much harm as the hot, heavy air of the room, which made her feel faint and giddy before she had breathed it five minutes.

Then she turned again towards him, put her hand on his shoulder, and looked into his face long and earnestly, while he fidgeted impatiently under the examination, repeating irritably—

"I'm all right, Deldee; I tell you I'm all right."

"You have broken your promise to me," said she reproachfully, without heeding his petulant protest.

"What promise? What promise?"

"The one you made to me in the garden at Waringham. I am not preaching at you now; it is too serious for that. There is a strange look in your eyes that frightens me. I believe—oh, James, I believe that you are killing yourself!"

"Nonsense!" said he, with an attempt at a laugh. "I tell you there is nothing the matter. I have a headache, that's all."

He got up, threw out his arms, stamped on the floor, and made an effort to pull himself together; but he shivered again, and, staggering, slipped back on to the chair from which he had risen. As he did so, his hands went up quickly to his head, and he gave a low exclamation of pain.

"I've got a splitting headache, and that's the truth!" he confessed, looking up at her and trying to speak brightly. "I've not been drinking, Deldee—is that what you mean?" he added, as the reason of her grave silence occurred to him.

"Then you have been taking some drug," said she authoritatively. "I am sure of it!"

"Well, don't be so angry. Yes; I've been taking morphine——"

"Why, that's poison, isn't it?" she interrupted, horror-struck.

"It is if you take enough of it; but I don't. It is used to lull pain and to give sleep——"

"But you shouldn't take it. You had better lie awake all night than doctor yourself like that. Why, if you were to take just a little too much of it, you might never wake up again!" cried Geraldine, in great excitement; and she thrust a bottle containing strong smelling-salts close to his nose with violent suddenness, which recalled to him her tyranny in their childhood, and set him coughing and choking and shedding unwilling tears. This result delighted her. "Now you'll be better!" she triumphantly declared; and, watching her opportunity, she applied her terrible remedy again.

But this time he snatched and retained it with an interjection which shocked her.

" I only did it for your good, you know," she explained gently, as she took out his pocket-handkerchief and affectionately dried his eyes.

"Yes, my dear child; but I would as soon be left to drag on a miserable existence as be killed outright for my good," he objected.

However, his very words showed that he was better; and Geraldine returned to the charge.

" Now you must promise me never to take morphine or anything of that sort any more," said she imperiously.

" I can't promise, so that settles it!" he answered doggedly. " Don't you see that I must know what I want better than you, Deldee? I don't take it unnecessarily or without advice. It is a doctor who prescribes it for me."

Geraldine remembered that the landlady had spoken of the doctor—spoken of him as another Mr. Hammond. A sense of the mystery which surrounded James and his strange mode of life came upon her again, and her imperious manner changed.

"Are you ill, then, James?" she asked anxiously.

"I have been ill; but I am better now, dear," he replied, drawing her arm round his neck and looking up at her affectionately. "Now tell me all about yourself."

"No, no, no; there is nothing to tell. I want to hear about you. When were you taken ill? How long have you been ill? Who——"

"One at a time, please. I had a fall nearly two months ago, when I had just come back to England from—from abroad. I don't quite know how it happened. I had been dining in town with a friend, and I fell down the stairs as we came out——"

"Ah!" interrupted Geraldine, shortly.

"No, I wasn't screwed; that is the astonishing part of it. I had drunk very little; yet, as I came out, I felt giddy and drowsy, and, as I tell you, I fell down the stairs. You don't believe me? Well, it doesn't matter; say I

was screwed, if you like.   At any rate, in my
fall I sprained my ankle, and—let me see, let
me see—I. was put into a cab insensible.   I
think I—I must have been insensible when
I fell, for I felt nothing at the time.   But
I must have hurt myself seriously, for since
then I have been subject from time to time to
the most violent pains.   I had an awful attack
last night—the worst I have ever had; if I
had been alone, I really think I should have
died.   Good Heavens, I can't bear to think
of it!"

He shuddered, and drew her hand more
closely round his neck.

" You ought to have had a doctor when you
fell," said Geraldine, whose face was eloquent
with sympathy and alarm.

"So I had.   It was a doctor I had been
dining with.   He can't think how it happened
himself, for, seeing that I couldn't walk steadily,
he had given me his arm."

"Why, he must have let you go!" cried
Geraldine, impetuously.

" He didn't mean to; I'll answer for it.   He
is my best friend—my only friend."

" Is that the man who calls himself your brother ? " she interrupted quickly.

James, who seemed to be growing drowsy and stupid again, raised his head and stared at her.

" Yes. How did you know ? "

" From the landlady. Who is he ? "

" I tell you—he is—my best friend—a friend who is—devoted to me. I owe him everything —everything ! "

His hand fell from hers, and his head slipped drowsily on to her shoulder.

" James, James ! Don't go to sleep again, James ! Wake up ! I am going away."

" Going away ! " he cried loudly, starting up in his chair and seizing her free hand. " No, no ; you must not go away ! I have thought of you and dreamt of you so often. Day after day and night after night I have seen you standing beside me as plainly as I see you now. You said you would come to me, you know— you said you would come—you said you would —come ! "

" And I kept my word, you see," she said, raising his head and speaking close to his ear to keep his failing attention. " Do you want me to come again, James ? Shall I come again ? "

" Don't go ! " he whispered back, clinging to her hands.

" But I must go, James. You know I have a husband now."

For a moment he looked puzzled, then he murmured—

" Oh, ah, yes, yes—of course, I remember ! " But her words evidently recalled no menace to his mind.

" Shall I come to-morrow and make the acquaintance of your brother, as you call him ? "

" Yes, do. Come and thank him for all he has done for me. What time will you come ? Come in the afternoon—will you ?—and I will get him to be here to meet you."

" Very well. I will be here about four to-morrow. Will that do ? "

" Yes. Don't be late; I shall live in a fever till the time comes, and I can see you again. Your face is always haunting me, and, now I have once really seen you and felt the touch of your hands, I shall not be able to rest without you.   You will come—you won't forget ? "

" Forget ! "   The tears were in her eyes, and in his too.

" You will kiss me, Geraldine ? "

Five minutes ago she would not have hesitated to do so; but those last wild words of his had frightened her, moved her out of herself.

" Kiss me ! " he repeated.

She stooped and put her lips to his cheek hurriedly, with a bright blush burning in her face.

" Good-bye ! " she whispered ; and, without daring to wait another moment, she fled out of the room and out of the house.

" Geraldine ! " he called, but she did not turn or answer.   And all the way to the station, all the way in the train, through every sound— the thud of the wheels, the noises of London —she had ringing still in her ears the cry— " Geraldine, Geraldine ! "

END OF VOL. II.

PRINTED BY WILLIAM CLOWES AND SONS, LIMITED,
LONDON AND BECCLES.   *G. C. & Co.*